Ray bent his head to kiss her deeply. Carrie tried to pull away, but desire won her over. His kiss, warm and inviting, settled deep in the pit of her stomach.

Carrie wanted more, she needed more, but common sense made her pull away. She was not ready to deal with the implications. "I think we should call it a night, Ray."

He pulled away slowly. "If you want." Running his finger gently down her cheek, he added, "I meant what I said tonight. I still love you as much now as when I saw you for the first time. Only this time, I'm not going to let you get away from me."

Pulling her jumbled thoughts together, Carrie stood up. "Ray, please don't say that. It's too late."

BOOK YOUR PLACE ON OUR WEBSITE AND MAKE THE ARABESQUE ROMANCE CONNECTION!

We've created a customized website just for our very special Arabesque readers, where you can get the inside scoop on everything that's going on with Arabesque romance novels.

When you come online, you'll have the exciting opportunity to:

- View covers of upcoming books
- Learn about our future publishing schedule (listed by publication month and author)
- Find out when your favorite authors will be visiting a city near you.
- Search for and order backlist books from our line catalog
- Check out author bios and background information
- Send e-mail to your favorite authors
- Join us in weekly chats with authors, readers and other guests
- Get writing guidelines
- AND MUCH MORE!

Visit our website at
http://www.arabesquebooks.com

FOREVER ALWAYS

JACQUELIN THOMAS

ARABESQUE

★BET BOOKS

BET Publications, LLC
www.msbet.com
www.arabesquebooks.com

ARABESQUE BOOKS are published by

BET Publications, LLC
c/o BET BOOKS
One BET Plaza
1900 W Place NE
Washington, D.C. 20018-1211

First Printing: March, 1999
10 9 8 7 6 5 4 3 2 1

Printed in the United States of America

DEDICATION

Carmellia Chavers

I really don't think any of this would be possible
if it wasn't for your constant show of support, your time,
your total honesty, and most of all—your friendship.

my friend, forever always

CHAPTER 1

"Mommy, Mommy, wake up! Wake up, Mommy."

"Huh? Wha—" Carrie muttered as she slowly awakened from a deep slumber. Recognizing her three-year-old son's voice through the foggy mist, she immediately sat upright. Pulling Mikey into her arms, Carrie held him close to her breast, making him feel safe and secure. As she lovingly massaged his small back, she asked, "What's wrong, Honey? What's the matter?"

Looking up, Mikey's wide eyes sought hers. "I skeared. I dreamed something was trying to get me. It was a bad man. He was real skeary, too."

"Ooh, Mikey." Carrie immediately gathered him deeper into her arms. "Honey, there's nothing to be scared of. I promise you, Baby, I won't let anything or anybody bother you. The house is all locked up. Remember?" When he nodded, she continued, "We locked all the doors and the windows together. Nobody is going to get in here. It's just you and me in the house, okay, Sweetie Pie?"

Mikey nuzzled against her, yawning. "Can I sleep in your bed, Mommy? I always feel safe in here with you."

"Of course you can." She smiled as he crawled off her lap and into her bed, clumsily snuggling under the covers.

"I love you, Mommy," he whispered sleepily.

She stared into his golden-brown eyes, so much like her own. Her son looked just like her, not resembling his father in any way.

Minutes later, Carrie stole a glance at her son, who now lay sleeping beside her, snoring softly. Her heart melted each time Mikey granted her a warm smile. He was such a loving child. Brushing her fingers lightly across his forehead, she smiled. Leaning over to kiss him softly, Carrie whispered, "I'm going to give you all my love, my sweet baby. I know you have no idea that you're the light of my life, but you are."

Carrie wished she could give him a little brother or sister, but that was not to be. Having another child meant getting involved with someone, and she intended to never let another man get that close to her again. Her relationship with Mikey's father not only taught her about herself, but about men in general.

In the last three and a half years, Carrie had done a lot of growing up. After Mikey was born, her life took on a new purpose. From the first moment she held Mikey in her arms, she felt a love like none she'd ever known. He looked so helpless, so tiny and fragile, all she'd wanted to do was protect him from all harm. His father dead, there was no one but the two of them. Carrie had resolved not to let her son suffer for his father's sins. Mikey didn't deserve that.

Tossing and turning in the heat of the July night, Carrie tried in vain to seek out the deep sleep that she had been taken from. Finally, she gave up. It was no use; she couldn't go back to sleep. It was all those thoughts of Martin, she admitted silently. Why did she fear him still? He was dead!

Easing gently from the bed, so as not to disturb her

small son, Carrie crept over to the window. Staring out, she peered up at the starlit night. Brunswick, Georgia became a fairly sleepy town when the sun went down. Looking up and down the street, Carrie noticed a sleek black car, which she'd never seen before, parked across from her tiny one-story brick house.

In the soft moonlight she could just barely make out the outline of a person in the car. Running her fingers through her light-brown hair, Carrie thought it odd that someone would be sitting out there at this time of night. Curiosity getting the better of her, she squinted to get a clearer look. What she saw caused a chill to run through her body, and she stumbled back toward the bed, stifling a scream.

Carrie gasped, panting in terror. "It can't be. Oh my God, it can't be," she whispered to herself over and over. While rubbing her arms to rid herself of the chill she was feeling, Carrie forced herself to take a deep, calming breath. Ignoring her shaking hands, the weak feeling in her legs that was turning them to jelly, and the sound of her heart pounding with deafening insistence in her ears, she squared her shoulders and stood up. She'd always counseled Mikey to face his fears head on—that it was just his imagination. Carrie vowed to do the same. Walking lightly across the room, she chanced another glance out her bedroom window. There was nothing. The car was gone. She'd never heard it drive away. Had a car really been out there in the first place? Carrie heard her son rustling in bed. She took one last look out of the window before joining Mikey in bed.

Was it just my imagination? Of course, it had to be. There was simply no other explanation. More than a little shaken, Carrie finally drifted off to sleep as the sun began its ascension into the heavens.

Los Angeles, California

Standing outside the courthouse on N. Hill street, John Sanders placed a firm hand on his client's shoulder. "Well, Ray, it's over now. Take my advice. Just count your blessings and move on. Lynette is out of your life."

Before Ray Ransom could respond, a soft lilting voice came from behind him.

"Ray, Honey, I'd like to talk to you before you leave, if you don't mind."

Ray grimaced and muttered, "Speak of the devil . . ." He swung his head around to look at his ex-wife. "What is it, Lynn?"

A beautiful woman of medium height, who was obviously pregnant, moved to stand in front of him. Her jet black hair flowed from a center part, falling to hang just below her chin. Looking pointedly at John, she said, "I'd like to speak with Ray alone, if you don't mind."

Ray looked up into John's warning gaze and nodded. "It's okay." Looking down, he scanned Lynette's smooth almond face, stopping on the living moistness of her full red mouth—a mouth that had given birth to six years worth of lies. Forcing himself to see past her beauty and her look of innocence, he asked, "What do you want?"

She suddenly looked nervous. "I just wanted to say that it didn't have to be this way, Ray. We could've had a happy marriage if you would've—"

"Don't try to blame me for this, Lynette," Ray interrupted. "We never should have gotten married in the first place." He shook his head sadly. "You just refused to admit the truth."

She gave his face, which was the color of warm chocolate, a soft stroking, pausing to trace the outline of his mustache. "You loved me once."

Ray stepped back to avoid her touch.

His action didn't seem to faze her. "You loved me until

you went to Georgia. I tried to be the kind of wife you wanted. I tried everything. You just stopped loving me—"

"I cared for you. I never said I was in love with you."

Tears filled Lynette's eyes. "I loved you, Ray. I loved you enough for the both of us. But we never had a fighting chance because of you. You never tried to save this marriage. NEVER."

Lynette pressed her lips together in anger, as if fighting to maintain her composure. Ray hated hurting her, but he had no choice. He should have been more honest with her in the beginning. Then they could have avoided all this pain. "I never lied to you, Lynn. You know the only reason I married you was because of the baby." His voice hardened. "A baby that never existed."

"And now you're divorcing me because of a baby." Lynette managed to reply through stiff lips. "A baby that does exist."

His face marked with loathing, Ray leaned forward and lowered his voice. "A baby that's not mine."

Lynette placed her hand on her protruding stomach. "This baby is yours, Ray. You're just too stubborn to admit it." Her coal-black eyes pierced the distance between them, and her expression grew hard and resentful. "How can you walk out on your child? How can you do this, Ray?"

He held up his hand. "We've been through this all before. I was born thirty years ago—not yesterday. I know it's not my baby. I can add, Lynn." Ray started to walk away. He stopped, turning back toward her. "Look, good luck . . . with everything. I've always tried to be honest with you. I—"

"Go to hell, Ray! I don't need you feeling sorry for me."

Raw hurt glittered in her dark eyes, causing Ray to feel guilty over his treatment of her. "Lynn—"

"Just leave me the hell alone." She started to walk away, but changing her mind, Lynette confronted Ray once more. Anger flashed in her eyes as she spoke. "What are you going to do now, Ray? Go find that tramp you've been pining for? If she's got half a brain, she'll have had the good sense to find herself a husband and forget all about you."

He shook his head sadly, his dark-brown eyes showing his regret. Sometimes she could be so vicious. "Don't worry about me. Just stay out of my life and I'll stay out of yours." Having said that, Ray turned and headed down the stairs. He heard her call him back but decided to ignore her. There was nothing more to be said.

John stood at the bottom of the stairs. Seeing the expression on Ray's face, he said, "If I were you, I'd stay away from her. She looks like she could kill you right about now."

Ray nodded his agreement. "She can be so sweet one minute and full of hatred the next."

John laughed. "I dated a woman like that once. Man, she tried to run me over one night."

Ray arched an eyebrow. "She actually tried to hit you with her car?"

John shook his head decisively. "Man, the woman was crazy with a capital C. You know I had to cut her loose."

"What did you do to tick her off?"

"I was seeing another woman and she caught me."

Ray laughed. "No wonder she tried to hit you. Messing around like that can definitely get you killed."

"Hey. What can I say? I'm a single man. I'm not looking for Mrs. Sanders. Not for a long time."

"I'd still be careful if I were you. You should be honest with the women you date," Ray warned his friend. "Some women don't take rejection lying down these days. They tend to want to inflict permanent damage to your body if you make them angry enough."

John stared pointedly at Ray. "Look where being honest has gotten you."

Ray simply shrugged.

As they neared Ray's green Lexus, the lawyer asked, "Have you thought about contacting the woman you were so in love with? The one you wanted to marry?"

"I should have married her. But she's probably happily married by now with a couple of kids." Ray pulled his keys out of his pants pocket and disarmed the car alarm.

"Maybe not. Why don't you check it out?"

Ray eased his six-foot frame into his car. "Even if she's not married, I would probably be the last person she'd want to see. I'm sure she must hate me for the way I treated her."

"If I were you, I'd look her up. Seems like the two of you have got some unfinished business."

Shaking his head, Ray said, "It's over. I made a mistake by leaving her the way that I did. I can't go back now."

John nodded his understanding. Switching his attaché case from his left to his right hand, he grinned. "Well, at least you finally got Lynette out of your life. Enjoy being single for a while. As a matter of fact, I've got a girl—"

Laughing, Ray shook his head. "That's okay, Buddy. The women you date are a little too kinky for me. I'm just an old-fashioned church-boy."

"Hey, don't knock it 'til you've tried it. But, all right, Church Boy. I forgot you like those sweet little girls who want families and a house with a white picket fence. Nowadays, you gotta damn near marry them just to go out to dinner with them."

"Actually, I think I'll stay away from women, period, for right now. I'm not looking for a wife, family, nothing. Lynn's antics are still too fresh in my mind. At this point, I don't think I'll ever get married again."

John waved away Ray's comments. "You will. You're the marrying type. You just need to find the right one. But you need a woman who can be a lady and a freak—"

Ray threw back his head, roaring with laughter. "Man,

I'll see you on Thursday. I've got to go. I'm meeting Garrick for dinner. We're celebrating my new-found freedom.''

"Tell your brother I said hello." John grinned wolfishly and added, "Jillian, too."

"Stay away from my sister. She's had enough men like you in her life."

John laughed. "Now, I could settle down with a woman like Jillian. I've just got to convince her that I'm not like all the others."

"That'll be the day . . ." Ray let the words hang in the air as he drove away.

Carrie was about to catch up on some much needed sleep when the phone rang. Intending to let the caller leave a message, she changed her mind and quickly picked up when she heard Brandeis's voice.

"Hello, Brandeis, I'm here." She stifled a yawn and stretched.

"Hi, Carrie. Were you busy?"

"No, I just got back from dropping Mikey off at my mother's house. She wanted to spend the day with him."

"Oh, I was hoping he was home. I wanted to talk to him."

Brandeis sounded so disappointed, Carrie suggested, "You can call him at my mom's." She quickly gave her the number. Forcing herself to sound cheerful, Carrie asked, "How is Brian?"

Brandeis obviously didn't buy her act, because she responded, "Carrie, is something wrong?"

When she tried to speak, Carrie's voice wavered. "No, why do you ask?"

"You don't sound like yourself. Are you sure you're okay?"

She could hear the concern in Brandeis's voice. "I'm fine. I've just been thinking a lot about Martin, though."

"That's understandable. That's another reason why I called. Lately, he's been on my mind, too. I don't know why, but I've started having dreams again."

Carrie glanced down at her nails. "You, too? Why is this happening now? Lord knows I've tried to forget."

"Carrie, we've got to stay strong. And you know if you need to talk, I'm here. We've both suffered a lot because of him."

Her teeth chattered and her body trembled. "C-can we change the subject, Brandeis? Martin's a mistake I'm really trying to forget. But then again, I've been trying for years to forget all the mistakes in my life."

"We certainly don't have to talk about him. As a matter of fact, I have something to tell you."

Carrie perked up. "What is it?"

"I've passed the bar and we're throwing a little dinner party on Saturday to celebrate. Jackson and I want you and Mikey to come up to Virginia next weekend. Mom, Carol, and James will all be here. Jackson and I want to buy the plane tickets for you and Mikey."

Carrie was deeply touched. "Are you sure you want me to come? I mean it's kind of a family celebration and all."

"Yes, Carrie. I want you to come," Brandeis stated firmly. "You and Mikey are part of our extended family."

"Great. We'll be there, like ants at a picnic. But Mikey and I will drive up. We'll leave early Friday evening."

"Are you sure you want to make the drive?"

"It's not really that bad. It gives Mikey and me a chance to spend quality time together as well as enjoy the scenery."

"Well, I'm looking forward to seeing you both."

"Thank you so much for inviting us." Carrie's mind drifted to the phantom sports car and its driver. "I think getting out of Brunswick for a few days is exactly what we need."

"Wonderful. I'd better go, but remember, if you need to talk, call me. I've got a hair appointment in forty-five minutes, but I wanted to speak to Mikey before I left, so I'd better give him a quick call."

"Take care, Brandeis. And thanks."

After hanging up the phone, Carrie ran outside just as she heard the postman drive away. Quickly retrieving the stack of neatly bundled envelopes of various sizes, she carried the mail into the house. While Carrie watched television, she scanned through the envelopes, until she came across a letter addressed to her from an accounting firm in Los Angeles. "Hmmmm, what's this?"

She quickly tore open the envelope while wondering what it could be about. She didn't know anyone in California.

Carrie quickly read over the contents, then read it once again more slowly. "I don't believe it. They're offering me a job." Reaching for the phone, she quickly dialed the phone number on the letterhead.

"Hello, may I speak to Robert Steele? This is Carrie McNichols."

An anonymous voice responded, "Just a moment please." Carrie hummed along with the jazzy tune that played while she waited. A deep, booming voice abruptly interrupted the music.

"This is Bob Steele. I see you received my letter, Ms. McNichols."

"Yes, I did. It arrived today. I'm just a little bit confused though. How did you come to contact me? I've never been to California, nor do I know anyone there. I don't remember talking to a recruiter."

He gave a deep chuckle. "A client of mine met you during his business dealings with Frank Matthews. He was very impressed by your professionalism. When he heard Frank was retiring, he called me, and raved nonstop about you. He said that Frank mentioned you had a degree in accounting."

She had just graduated earlier this year. "If you don't

mind my asking, who is this client? He seems to know an awful lot about me."

"My client prefers to remain anonymous."

Carrie frowned. She wasn't sure how she felt about this. "I see."

"Would you want it known that you're the reason a valued employee is stolen from her company?"

She thought about this for a moment. "No, I guess not." Carrie had been contemplating a job change for months now—but California? How would Mikey feel about such a move? Bob Steele's words cut through her reverie.

"Well, what do you say? Will you at least come out for a visit to see if you'd be interested? I have an opening for a junior accountant."

"If you don't mind, I'd like to think about it. I'll call you in a few days."

"I look forward to hearing from you, Ms. McNichols."

Carrie hung up, wondering who the mysterious person could be. Finally, exhausted from too little sleep, she turned off the TV and stretched out on her couch, closing her eyes.

After her nap, Carrie felt totally refreshed and decided to do a little shopping. She ran a few errands before heading to the Glynn Place Mall. Her first stop was Belk-Hudson. In the dress department, she selected a few items before strolling to the dressing rooms.

Carrie disrobed silently, while she concentrated on next week's dinner menu. She planned to go grocery shopping when she left the mall. Having selected a dress, she was just about to exit the stall when the voices in the next stall caught her attention.

"Girl, you won't believe who I thought I saw come into Belk's a short time ago."

"Who, Freda?" the other voice responded.

"Your coworker—Miz McNichols."

"You serious?"

"Yeah. I think she's somewhere over by the children's department. That's where I saw the tramp."

Carrie held her anger in check. Lily was in the very next stall with her sister. She and Lily hadn't spoken to each other in the last year or so, other than to exchange small pleasantries during business hours.

"She sure has gotten real uppity since she had that baby. Does she even talk to you anymore?" Freda asked.

"No, she don't say much to nobody these days. She's all buddy buddy with Brandeis now. But I remember when she wanted Jackson and every other man Brandeis had. Look how she hooked up with that Martin. I knew from the get-go that he was bad. Pretty men like that—nothing but trouble. All he was doing was just using Carrie to get Brandeis. I heard she even got pregnant on purpose to keep him. Didn't work though. Now, she ought to know by now that having a baby don't keep no man."

"Humph, as far as I'm concerned, she ain't nothing but a slut anyway. All she did was give it up to anybody that wanted it—even that fool. I heard he raped Brandeis. That's why he kidnapped her. They tried to keep it all quiet, but word got out."

"Carrie thinks she's as good as Brandeis, but she isn't. Brandeis always had class—Carrie doesn't."

Tears streamed down her face as she listened to Lily's and Freda's vicious words. It wasn't the first time she'd heard those sentiments cast about her, but it didn't lessen the pain.

"Well, I'm glad I don't have to work with her. I'd have to tell the bitch something. Whether she knows it or not, she ain't all that."

"Freda, I don't even worry about Carrie. I can't let her work my nerves. If she don't want to talk to me—so be it. She's the one running around all alone now. Been through all the men in this town and through FLETC. I swear she knows almost every single man out at the Federal Law Enforcement Training Center. Don't nobody want her now. But see, I got a man. And girl, he really keeps me busy. All Carrie got is Mikey. Now I have to admit, he's a cute little boy . . .''

Carrie didn't hear any more of Lily's comments, because she'd quietly eased out of the dressing room and left the store as quickly as she could. She didn't stop driving until she was in the driveway of her house. By the time she was inside, Carrie had decided to travel to Los Angeles.

She called Bob Steele the next day and made arrangements to fly out in two weeks.

CHAPTER 2

Arlington, Virginia

Mona walked gracefully into the den carrying a pitcher of lemonade. "Well, hello, Carrie. How are you doing? You were sleeping when I checked on you earlier. I was pleased to see you resting after that long drive."

Carrie looked up from the magazine she had been reading. "I'm fine, Mrs. Taylor. I've been meaning to call you, but I've been so busy."

Settling down next to Carrie, Mona poured the iced cold liquid into a glass and offered it to her. "Oh, don't worry about me, Dear. I know with working and raising your son, you probably have little time for yourself."

Carrie accepted the glass. "I'm embarrassed that we live in the same small town, and I barely see you. Actually, I see you more here in Virginia then I do in Georgia."

"That's because she is in Virginia more than she is in Georgia. I keep trying to persuade her to move up here," Jackson's voice boomed from behind them. "Hello, Carrie.

It's good to see you. Where's Mikey?'' He leaned down to kiss Mona on her cheek, then Carrie.

"He's already dressed and upstairs playing with Brian.''

Jackson grinned. "There's no telling what those two are up to. Maybe I'd better go check on them.''

"They were getting dressed last I checked and Bran is up there with them.'' Mona patted the empty space next to her. "Why don't you come sit and keep Carrie company? I need to press my clothes for tonight.''

Jackson sat down on the loveseat facing Carrie. Pouring himself a glass of lemonade, he smiled and asked Carrie, "How are you doing? You seemed a little preoccupied earlier.''

She returned his smile. "I'm making it. It gets really hard when Mikey starts talking about his father. He wants to know everything about him. I try to think of the good in Martin, but . . . well, I don't want to lie to my son.'' Tears glittered in her eyes. "Mikey even asked me once if his daddy loved him.''

"What did you say?''

Carrie stared down at her hands. "I lied to him. What else could I do? I told him Martin loved him. Loved him to death.''

Pushing his glasses up, Jackson nodded. "You did the right thing. We don't really know what was going through his mind. Martin had some serious problems, but it's hard to imagine him not loving his own flesh and blood.''

Carrie nodded. She brushed away her tears. "Not for me. He was crazy.''

"Who's crazy?'' Brandeis walked slowly into the room. Jackson stood to assist her. She limped slightly, due to the car accident that had killed Martin. Noting Carrie's expression, she stated, "You two were talking about Martin.''

When she was seated, Jackson sank down beside her. "Mikey's been asking about him.''

Brandeis peered over at Carrie. "Oh, just tell him enough to satisfy his curiosity," she suggested.

"That's what I've been doing. I just hope it won't come back to haunt me."

"I understand, but what else can you tell him? He's so young."

"I hate lying to him. I feel like an awful mother—"

"You're a good mother, Carrie—just love him. Mikey'll be all right," Jackson commented.

"I hope so." She watched the loving exchange between Jackson and Brandeis. Here was a couple who'd truly gone through hell and back, but together, they had kept their marriage intact. They were so much in love. "Brandeis, I like your dress. It's beautiful."

Jackson nodded his agreement.

"Thanks. It was a gift from Mom."

"She is a remarkable seamstress."

"Don't you sew, Carrie?" Brandeis asked as she helped herself to a glass of lemonade.

"I sew, but not like that. I can only make very simple things."

Brandeis raised a perfectly arched eyebrow. "You're just being modest. I've seen some of the clothes you made for Mikey. They're lovely. I also love the comforter set you made for Brian when he was a baby. We still have it, you know."

"You're kidding." Deep inside, Carrie was truly touched.

Brandeis shook her head. "It's a beautiful keepsake."

Jackson stood. "I'd better check on the boys and your mother." Pushing his glasses up, he glanced down to check his watch. "By the way, where are James and Carol? We need to leave shortly."

Brandeis set her glass down on a nearby table. "Honey, I forgot to tell you. They're going to meet us at the restaurant. Their plane was late getting in, and James had a business meeting with a client in D.C."

"How is Carol doing with her pregnancy?" Carrie wanted to know.

Brandeis reached up and pinched Jackson on the arm when he laughed. Seeing Carrie's questioning gaze, she explained, "She's fine. Jackson just thinks Carol eats everything in sight. He teases her about it all the time."

"Well, she does," he agreed. "She looks good though. Not as big as I thought she'd be for as much as she eats."

"Pregnant women are eating for two, Jackson. You should be ashamed of yourself." Carrie wagged her finger at him. "I declare, I can't believe you'd tease the poor thing like that. Women are sensitive about the way they look when they're pregnant."

"She knows I'm kidding, doesn't she?" A seemingly worried Jackson looked to his wife for the answer.

Brandeis merely shrugged. "Well, she doesn't cry anymore, if that's what you mean." She winked her eye at Carrie.

Jackson looked stricken. "She cried?"

Brandeis and Carrie glanced over at each other and burst out laughing.

"Honey, I was only teasing you."

"I'm going to check on the kids."

"Jackson . . ." This time it was Brandeis who looked stricken.

He stopped at the door and winked. "Two can play this game."

Brandeis wrinkled her nose at him.

Looking from one to the other, Carrie laughed. "You two are crazy."

Forty-five minutes later, they arrived at the restaurant. Carol and James had arrived before them and were already seated.

Mikey rushed to plant a kiss on Carol's cheek. "Hey, Auntie Carol." Pointing to her protruding belly, he asked, "When's the baby coming out?"

Carol laughed. "Hi, cutie. The baby's due in ten weeks."

Mikey frowned. "Awwww, that baby sure is taking a long time to come. I think maybe he likes it in there and won't never come out."

Carol placed a hand to her mouth to stifle her laughter.

Pulling Mikey by the arm, Carrie led him to the chair next to where she was going to sit. "Hi, Carol, James. Come here, Honey. Let's take a seat right over here."

Mikey gently pulled away. "I wanna sit next to Brian, Mommy."

Carrie placed a gentle, but firm, hand on his shoulder "Honey, Mommy wants you to sit next to her."

He shook his head. "I don't want to . . ."

More firmly, she said, "Mikey, you need to sit beside me. I have to help you with your food."

"No, you don't. I wanna sit by—"

"Mikey . . ." Carrie pointed to the chair next to hers.

"I don't wanna sit here . . ." Mikey whined as he slumped into the chair and started to pout.

Jackson placed Brian in the seat on the other side of Mikey. "Brian's right next to you. You shouldn't give your mom such a hard time, Mikey."

Mikey looked up at Carrie. "I still love you, Mommy. I just wanna sit next to my godbrother. He's the bestest friend I got."

She leaned over and kissed him on the forehead. "I know, Baby. But you're my best friend, too."

As soon as everyone was seated, the waiter brought over a bottle of sparkling apple cider and a bottle of champagne. Carrie noticed Brandeis accepted only the apple cider tonight. After Jackson gave a toast to his wife, chilled plates laden with leaves of lettuce, tomatoes, and cucumbers were delivered to the table.

Throughout dinner, Carrie watched Brandeis. It was so amazing that after all she had been through, she was still so beautiful, inside and out. She was able to finish law school, pass the bar exam, and had actually put on a few pounds. She looked so happy that she was actually glowing . . . a smile tugged at Carrie. Putting her fork down, Carrie asked, "Jackson, aren't you forgetting something?"

He looked perplexed for a moment. "What?"

She looked pointedly at Brandeis. "He does know, doesn't he?"

Comprehension dawned, and Brandeis shook her head.

Jackson looked from one woman to the other. "What are you two talking about? What should I know?"

Mona pointed her fork toward Jackson. "It seems to me that you're going to have another baby."

Jackson's mouth dropped open.

Brandeis placed her hand over his. "I guess my secret's out. I was going to tell you tonight."

"Oh, Brandeis, I'm so sorry for opening my big mouth."

"It's okay, Carrie."

Brian tugged on his father's sleeve. "Mama's having a baby?"

Jackson's grin spread ear to ear. "Yeah, Son. Mama's having a baby. You're going to have a little brother or sister."

"I want a baby sister. Don't want a brother." Brian folded his hands across his chest as he sat back in his chair.

"Why not?" Brandeis wanted to know.

" 'Cause I have Mikey, and Auntie Carol's baby is a boy." He pointed to himself, saying, "I want me a sister!"

"Now, Dear, we have to be thankful for whatever the good Lord gives us. You may have a little brother," Mona intervened. "And he's going to need his big brother a lot."

"I'm sure you're going to be a good brother to this baby, boy or girl," Brandeis stated.

He wrinkled his nose before muttering, "I guess a little brother is fine."

Mona dabbed at her mouth daintily with her napkin.

"Oh, dear. Not him, too. I was so hoping that he'd outgrow that nasty little habit—seeing as his mother didn't."

Jackson leaned over and kissed Brandeis. "I think it's cute."

Brandeis wrinkled her nose at Mona.

Laughter burst out all around the table.

Carrie was exhausted. Last weekend they had been in Virginia, and for the last three days, she'd been in California. Bob Steele and his employees were very hospitable. After meeting him, she'd decided to take the job. He had even assisted in finding a place for her and Mikey to live. They would be moving to Los Angeles within two weeks. Although a little nervous about making such a big move, Carrie found herself looking forward to the change.

Bone-weary, she drove from the airport to her mother's house. Using her key, Carrie unlocked the old, weathered front door. Just as she stepped into the living room, she heard tiny footsteps running across the hardwood floor. Carrie dropped her bags near the sofa and stood with her hands wide open.

"Mommy, Mommy, I'm so glad you're back." Mikey jumped on Carrie, knocking her down on the sofa. "I thought you weren't never coming back from Californy." He hugged her tightly, planting wet kisses all over her face. "I missed you."

"Whoa, honeychile! Slow down." She sat him on her lap as she settled back on the sofa. "I missed you, too. You knew I was coming back, because I called you every single night and told you so." Running her fingers through his sandy-brown curls, Carrie smiled. "I would never leave you, Sweetheart."

"I'm glad you came home. I didn't like it when you were gone."

"Didn't you have fun here with Grandma?"

"Yeah, but it wasn't the same 'cause you weren't here. I wanted you. Don't leave me again, Mommy."

"I won't, Sweetheart. I won't."

"Are we moving to Californy?"

Carrie nodded. "It's a good opportunity for us. We're moving to California." She pronounced it slowly. "How do you feel about leaving your preschool and Grandma?"

"We can come back to visit, cain't we?"

"We sure can."

"Mommy, can we go home now? I wanna go home and pack up my toys. I got lots to tell you."

"Sure, Baby. Let me go talk to Grandma for a few minutes, okay?"

"Okay. I'm gonna go get my backpack." He was running as fast as his little stubby legs would carry him.

"Whew! Hey, Carrie, Honey. How was your trip?"

Carrie stood up to give her mother a hug. "Hey, Mama. The trip was good. I decided to take the job. I also found an apartment. It's not too far from the office and there's a preschool a couple of blocks from where we'll be staying."

"That's wonderful, Baby." Mrs. McNichols patted her ample bosom. "Lordy, I have to tell ya, I'm glad you home. That youngun of yours plum near drove me crazy with all his worrying about you."

"I missed him too, Mama. We've never been separated before."

"I know."

Carrie assisted her mother as she settled down on the couch. She was still panting hard. "Are you exercising like you should? You still get out of breath too quick, Mama."

"I'll be fine. I just been running a lot today—"

"You need to slow down." Carrie sat down next to her mother.

Ethel panted loudly. "Chile, I know you not talking about me. You're the one that needs a break. You're so wrapped up in your baby—and you can't do that. You haven't been out socially since Martin." She shook her head. "Huh. I remember when nothing could keep you from a man . . . yeah, you sure was crazy about men."

Carrie winced at her mother's words. "Those days are over. I have Mikey and he's my priority."

"Mikey sure has changed you, Chile."

Carrie smiled. "Yes, but it wasn't just Mikey. It was me— I didn't like me very much. Most of all it was because of my son. To him, I can do no wrong." She laughed. "He thinks I'm smart, I'm wonderful—basically just the next best thing to peanut butter."

"He loves you something fierce, that's for sure."

"And I'm not going to do anything to change his opinion of me."

Ethel patted Carrie's hand. "You're a good mama, Chile. You really are. I'm proud of you."

"Mama, you were, too. There was just too many of us, I think."

"I did the best I could . . . you knew I loved you, didn't you? Your daddy, Lord rest his soul, worked himself into the grave, trying to feed and clothe this family. I had to raise the nine of you all by myself cause he worked all the time."

"I guess I wanted people to like me—care about me, but all I ended up with was a bad reputation."

"Remember something, Baby. They talked about Jesus Christ. You made some bad choices in your life, but don't go round with your head hanging low—stand up straight and proud."

"I'm leaving because I don't want Mikey exposed to my past. And in a town this small . . ." Carrie shook her head.

"I know, Baby. That's why I said what I did. Ever since that U. S. Marshal—"

"I don't want to talk about him."

"You loved him, Chile. I believe you still do. Matter of fact, I think you used to go from man to man because you were trying to forget, but I'm here to tell you—that's not the way."

"I know, Mama. That's another reason why I'm not in any hurry to date. I'm not ready. I don't think I'll ever be."

Los Angeles, California

Weary, Carrie parked in a space underneath a mammoth peach-colored apartment building and turned off the car. Running her fingers through her son's curly hair, she announced, "This is it, Honeychile. This is where we're going to live."

"Wow, Mommy, this building is huge."

Carrie got out of the car, then proceeded to help Mikey out. Pointing to a paisley-print overnight bag, she said, "Grab that bag over there—the one with your toys. We're going to take that stuff upstairs now."

They entered the building and headed to the manager's office. Thirty minutes later, the two were on the elevator, en route to their new home. Arriving at the eighth floor, they exited and walked toward their new apartment.

Mikey's eyes widened at the vast apartment. "Mommy, this place is big." Running to the fireplace, he said, "Boy! We have a fireplace just like the one in Brian's house. Now Santa can come down the chimney. He won't have to use the front door no more."

Carrie shook her head and laughed. "Come on. Let's see your room." Mikey rushed over and placed his tiny hand in hers. He jumped up and down at the sight of his room. "We could put our old house in this room."

"Mikey, this room is not that big. It's larger than the one we left, but our whole house couldn't fit in here."

Mikey was not convinced. "I bet it can. Can I have some bunk beds in here? That way Brian can sleep here, too."

Carrie rubbed her hand through his hair. "You sure

can, Honey. We're going to go shopping for them on Saturday. For right now though, we're going to have to sleep in the sleeping bags we brought with us."

Mikey glanced up at her. "Why did you sell all our furniture, Mommy?"

"Since we're starting a new life here, I thought we'd start it with all new furniture, too."

"Oh." Mikey was quiet for a moment. "Where's your room?"

"Right down the hall. I'll show you." Carrie stopped briefly at another door. "See. You even have your own bathroom."

"I have my own bathroom?"

"You sure do."

Mikey glanced around. "But where is yours?"

"In my bedroom." She opened the door, holding it to let Mikey inside. He walked around the room, peering into the huge walk-in closet, the master bath area, and out the window. Turning to her, he grinned and said, "I like this place."

Carrie returned his grin with one of her own. "I like it, too. Now come on. We have to unpack the car. We're not going to worry about the heavy boxes. We'll just get the things we need for right now."

"Okay, Mommy."

Half an hour later, Carrie said, "I'm going to start unpacking some of this stuff. Why don't you go into your room and play?"

"You don't want me to help you? I can help."

"I know, Sweetie. Hey, I know how you can help me."

"How?"

"Why don't you open your suitcase and take out your clothes. Put your socks in one pile, your underwear in another."

"Okay, want me to hang up the other clothes?"

Carrie bit back a smile. "I don't think you're tall enough

just yet. I'll hang them up for you." She stood in the doorway watching her son for a few minutes before resuming her own unpacking. She was glad to be away from Brunswick, Georgia. Los Angeles promised to be the beginning of a new life for her and Mikey. Feeling a peace she hadn't known in a long time, she happily embraced the future.

Excited by the new apartment, Mikey ventured from room to room. First, he checked out the kitchen. Satisfied, he headed back to his room, but catching sight of the slightly open front door, he veered in its direction.

Unable to resist taking a peek out, he stuck his head into the hallway. Mikey was soon running down the long hallway to the elevators. Turning right, he headed back up the corridor. This time he turned and ran in the opposite direction. Confused, he looked from door to door. They all were identical. Frightened, Mikey headed back in the direction of the elevators.

CHAPTER 3

Ray keyed in his security code and waited for the sound of the familiar buzzing that would unlock the front entry of his apartment building. He'd decided not to park in the garage since he planned to be home only long enough to change clothes and water the plants in his sister's apartment. Since he'd moved into the same building, he'd become her offical plant waterer whenever she traveled.

As soon as he pushed the button to summon one of the four elevators, the one closest to his left opened. He was met by a teary-eyed little boy. Ray estimated him to be about three to four years of age. Although he had never seen him before, he seemed familiar somehow.

"Hello, little one. Why so sad?"

"I cain't find my mommy."

"My name is Ray. What's your name?"

"Michael, but everybody calls me Mikey."

"Can I call you Mikey?"

He sniffled before answering. "Y-yeah." Mikey started crying harder.

Ray dropped his briefcase and scooped the crying child

into his arms. "Whoa, little fella. It's going to be okay. I'll help you find your mother." *And when I do, I'm going to tell her a thing or two,* he silently fumed. Didn't she have a clue what could happen to a young child roaming around like this?

"Do you know where you live?"

Mikey shook his head.

"What is your mother's name? And your daddy's?" Ray silently cursed the little boy's parents. The apartment manager lived on the same floor as he did. Hopefully, he would be able to locate Mikey's parents.

"Her name is Caroline. My daddy died. We just moved here to Californy."

"I see. I'm sorry to hear about your daddy. So you're new in this building, huh?" He decided that maybe blasting Mikey's mother would not be such a good idea after all. She was probably deep in her grief over losing her husband.

"I want my mommy, Ray."

"I know, Son. I know. I'm going to find her, I promise."

As they traveled up to the eighth floor, Mikey called his name softly. "Ray?"

"Yes?"

"I skeared."

The little boy started to cry again. Ray held him tighter. "Don't be scared, Mikey. I won't let anything happen to you."

Finally, Mikey's tears subsided and Ray put him down.

"Do you h-have any kids?"

Ray was silent for a moment. "No. No, I don't."

"Do you want kids?"

"Sure, I want kids, lots of them."

"Then will you be my daddy forever always?"

Ray tried to think of an appropriate response, but the elevator stopped on his floor, and the opening of the doors saved him from having to answer Mikey right then.

* * *

"Mikey?" Carrie called from the kitchen. "Where are you? You're much too quiet." She paused and waited for an answer. Hearing none, she called once more. "Where are you, Honeychile?" Again she was met by silence. A tiny thread of fear began to creep through her body. Where was Mikey?

Dropping the box containing Tupperware, she ran from room to room, looking for her son.

"This is not funny, Mikey. It's not nice to scare your mommy like this, Honey. Come on out, now." She chanced a look at the front door. "Oh my God! Mikey." Carrie ran toward the elevator. She paced back and forth as she waited. Growing impatient by the minute, she was just about to take the stairs when the doors opened and a little boy walked out.

"Mikey!" she cried with relief. "Where on earth have you been? I've been looking for you like crazy." She pulled him into her arms and held him close to her breast, not looking up once at the other occupant on the elevator. "I've told you about taking off on your own, Honeychile. You can't do that. I was so scared." Carrie covered his tawny face with kisses. "I'm so glad you're okay."

Honeychile? He hadn't heard that particular endearment since he was in Brunswick, Georgia. Ray looked at the petite woman kneeling down as she talked to Mikey. He stared long and hard. Could it be?

"Carrie?" Ray did not realize he had said her name aloud.

She heard her name called and noticed the tall, slender man standing near the elevator.

"Hello, Carrie . . . how . . . uh . . ." He cleared his throat. Recognition dawned on her pixielike features—recognition, followed by an expression of utter shock, which further stilled his lips.

While he stood there, awkwardly searching for words of greeting, Carrie's medium-brown eyes opened wide. Tears glimmered on their surface. Ray wanted to touch her, to comfort her, or at least to offer her a smile, but she looked as though she were seeing a ghost.

Ray tried again. "How are you?"

"YOU!" Anger contorted her face. Before he could say another word, she grabbed Mikey by the arm, and started to walk away.

"Oww, Mommy. You're hurting my arm."

Carrie kneeled once again until she faced her son. "I'm sorry, Baby."

"Mommy, Ray's my friend. He's gonna be my—"

Standing up with her back straight, Carrie glared up at Ray. "Stay away from my son," she instructed in a no-nonsense tone he was tempted to obey.

"Carrie—"

"As a matter of fact, stay away from the both of us." She backed away slowly as he neared them.

Seeing the flurry of emotions on her face, Ray retreated and put a bit more distance between them. He'd figured she might not be too happy to see him again, but he would've never guessed she'd be this angry. "Wait a minute, Carrie. We need to talk."

Giving him a scorching look, Carrie was not in the least bit interested in anything he had to say. Instead, she turned to Mikey and said, "Come on, Honey. We've still got a lot of unpacking to do."

"Mommy, how do you know Ray? Is he your friend?"

"No, he is definitely not a friend of mine." Her voice was tinged with menace.

Mikey stopped walking. "Why don't you like him? He's—"

"Honey, Mommy was very worried about you. You know

you shouldn't run out of the apartment like that. It's not safe, and if you do it again, you're going to be punished. Understand?"

"Yes." Mikey was quiet for a moment. "Mommy?"

"Yes, Honey."

"Why?"

"Why what?"

"How come it's not safe?"

She regarded Ray with cold speculation and stated, "There are some very bad people around. People that will hurt you."

Ray straightened a notch. What in the hell did she think he would do to the little boy? Then he realized she hadn't been talking about Mikey. She was referring to herself. As she and Mikey walked down the long corridor, he watched her closely. The sight of him had shaken her to her toes, that was obvious. And although seeing her had done the same to him, he was fully aware that their two reactions were as opposite as day and night.

Even with no trace of make-up, faint shadows under her eyes, and her long, golden-brown hair pulled back in a ponytail, Carrie was still as beautiful as he remembered. She wore a pair of torn and faded blue jeans with a sweatshirt. Ray decided then and there that if he never did anything else in his life, he was going to make up for all the hurt he had caused her in the past. Somehow, some way, he would make amends for breaking her heart.

While undergoing thirteen weeks of rigorous training at the Federal Law Enforcement Training Center, with the U.S. Marshals, Ray had spotted her one Saturday at a theater in Brunswick. From the moment he laid eyes on her, Ray wanted her in a way he'd never wanted another woman. He'd gone straight over and introduced himself. After that, they'd spent every possible moment together. Something instantaneous and magical had sparked between them. Even now, he still felt that spark where she was concerned.

As Carrie neared her apartment, she turned to see if he was still behind them. Her face hardening, she stopped and faced him. "Why are you following us, Ray?"

"I see not much has changed since the last time I saw you. You're still vain. However, for your information, I'm not following you. I'm going to my apartment. I happen to live in this building, on this floor."

Embarrassed, Carrie turned and began walking at a faster pace. Ray watched with interest as she neared his apartment. She stopped at the apartment right before his. Carrie's going to be living right next door, he thought. His heart skipped a beat. This is going to be interesting!

Carrie heard the door to the apartment next to hers open. Dear God, it couldn't be. Ray lives right next door. Would this nightmare ever end? He would be sleeping next door. Lord help her, the idea left her lightheaded . . . and angry. Forcing her thoughts to the situation at hand, Carrie examined Mikey thoroughly. His overalls hung on his chubby frame by one strap; the other one dangled down his back. "What happened to your button?"

Mikey's eyes flashed. She could tell he was about to burst with some sort of news.

"Where is your button, Honeychile?"

"I losted it," he explained in a plaintive tone. "Mommy, I got something to tell you." His voice gained volume, and with it, excitement. His round eyes widened. "I found me a daddy."

"Oh, honey, you can't just go out and find a daddy."

Mikey was persistent. "But, Mommy—"

"Let's get you undressed. Mommy will explain how getting a daddy works."

"But I want this daddy. The one I founded."

"You already have a daddy, Sweetheart. He's in hea—, he's with the ang . . . uh—" Carrie tried to think of something to tell her small son. She couldn't tell him that Martin was surely in hell, paying for his crimes.

"My daddy's sleeping. He's sleeping 'til God calls him up to heaven for Judgment Day," Mikey said proudly.

Carrie was stunned. "Where on earth did you hear that?"

He grinned. "Grandma told me that."

"Well, she's absolutely correct." Thank you, Mama, I owe you one, she thought.

"Mommy, some of my friends got more than one daddy. I want me one, too."

Carrie thought her heart would break. She pulled him into her arms. "I know, Baby."

"I been a good boy. I deserve one. I been a real good boy, haven't I, Mommy?"

Carrie's arms trembled, and tears brimmed in her eyes. She fought valiantly to keep Mikey from seeing either. "Yes, my precious sweetheart. You've been a very good boy. Mommy loves you so much and I'm so proud of you. I don't know what I'd do without you in my life."

"So, can I have a daddy?"

Carrie released a deep sigh. "It's not that simple. You see, Mommy has to meet someone. Then we fall in love and get married, and he'll be your daddy."

"I want Ray to be my daddy," Mikey kept insisting. "You already know him, Now all you have to do is fall in love and get married. I love Ray, don't you?"

Brows furrowed, Carrie ran delicate fingers through Mikey's curls. "Honey, it's time for your bath."

"But, Mommy . . ."

"No buts. It's time to take a bath. After you get cleaned up, I'll make you a sandwich and some warm milk. That should help you sleep."

"Will you tell me a bedtime story while I drink my milk?"

"Of course, Honey."

"Can I go see Ray tomorrow?"

"Ray is a very busy man. I don't know that he'll be home." Carrie knew that seeing Ray was the last thing she wanted to do. Mikey, on the other hand, seemed enthralled with him.

"We can knock on his door and see."

"I suppose we could. Let Mommy think about it, okay?"

"Okay. Mommy?"

"Yes, Sweetie."

"Ray says he wants lots of children. He loves children."

"Take off those dirty clothes. Right this minute, young man."

Mikey giggled as she tickled him.

Carrie quickly bathed him and put him to bed. He fell asleep before she finished reading him his favorite story. She kissed him on his cheek and tiptoed out of his room.

She decided to get the last of the boxes out of the trunk of her car. After two trips upstairs, Carrie rushed down a final time to retrieve the last box of their belongings. It was heavier than she remembered. Just as she was struggling to remove it from the car, Carrie felt someone lift it from her arms. She was about to say thanks until she saw who it was. Frowning, she snapped, "What do you want, Ray?"

Carrie's tone held no trace of appreciation, clearly indicating that Ray would not be getting any thanks.

"I was just trying to help. You seemed to be struggling with the box."

"I can manage without your help."

He responded with a shrug before walking away.

Carrie resisted the urge to call him back for help. Cursing her foolish pride, she struggled with the heavy box until she finally sat it on top of the car. Feeling eyes on her, she glanced around and saw Ray watching her.

Shaking his head, Ray headed toward Carrie. Without saying a word, he picked up the box and carried it inside the apartment building, while Carrie stood by speechless.

He had gotten on an elevator and was gone by the time

Carrie made it inside. When she reached the eighth floor, she found he'd left the box outside her door and was nowhere to be found. After dragging the box inside, she found a piece of paper, tape, and a pen. She scribbled a quick note of thanks and stuck it on his front door.

Carrie didn't sleep much that night, what with everything that had transpired during the day—the most significant of which was the move to California. The most disturbing thing had been seeing Ray Ransom again.

Ray looked exactly as she remembered. And boy, did she remember. That was the trouble. She had remembered for a while. His goodlooking features were chiseled in warm milk chocolate. Even now, Ray still wore his hair cut close, giving him a youthful appearance. Although he stood tall and slender, his muscles bulged beneath his shirt. And of course, Carrie couldn't forget his sexy high hips. Memories haunted her—memories at once both poignant and despicable. Carrie got out of bed, went to stand at the window, as was her habit when she couldn't sleep, and stared into the starry night. She leaned against the wall, hugging herself and squeezing her eyes shut, attempting in vain to clear her head of the dreadful fact that she had not forgotten Ray. Or the way that he had once made her feel.

She had learned to hate him, yes. Her brain knew him for the dog he was, but her body hadn't forgotten the magic. Seeing him brought it back with such force, her skin prickled. Carrie curled her lips together, not wanting to remember, but was unable to forget.

Lord, that woman was stubborn. Stubborn and proud. Ray bit back his laughter when he recalled how comical she'd looked trying to carry that box, laden with her possessions. Even he'd had a time carrying it. What in the world had she packed in it—it felt like a ton of bricks. Ray wondered how she'd even gotten it in the car.

Carrie was his neighbor. Ray shook his head—he couldn't believe it. It was good seeing her again after all this time. He never in a million years thought that he'd ever see Carrie again. Perhaps he could find a way to make things right between them. He had his work cut out for him, however. He knew Carrie would not make it easy.

Ray had to admit she had every right to hate him. He'd led her to believe they could have a future together, and then he'd turned around and told her that he was engaged to be married. For weeks after that, Ray couldn't rid himself of the guilt he felt over hurting Carrie.

Hearing the phone, Ray answered on the third ring. "Hello."

"Ray, I need you to come over. I'm scared."

"Lynn, what's wrong?"

"I think someone's trying to break into the house. Please come over here."

"Did you call the police?"

"I called them twenty minutes ago. Ray, I'm scared . . ." She started to cry.

"I'll be right there." Ray stood up and reached for his keys. He headed for the door.

As he passed Carrie's apartment, he wondered if she and Mikey had settled in okay.

Ray drove quickly, arriving at the house he used to share with Lynette. Outwardly, everything looked normal. He approached with caution. After a thorough check around the house, he knocked on the door.

"What on earth took you so long, Ray? I could've been killed," Lynette admonished. "Is that what you'd hoped?"

Ray took in his ex-wife's state of undress. Gesturing to the sheer black lace peignoir set, he asked, "Is that what you wear when you think someone is breaking in?"

Lynette moved aside to let Ray enter the house. "I wasn't thinking about how I looked—I was afraid, Ray."

"I expected to find the police here. Have they come already?"

"No, they never showed up." Lynette moved toward the living room. "I need to sit down."

Ray followed her. She moved over to make room for him on the love seat, but Ray chose to sit in the recliner situated near the marble fireplace.

"I checked around the house, Lynn. I didn't find evidence of anyone trying to break in."

"I heard something or somebody out there." She sounded defensive. "You think I'm lying, don't you?"

"I didn't say that, Lynn. I'm simply saying that I don't think you have anything to worry about." Ray stood up. "I don't know why the police haven't shown up yet. It's been an hour since you called, right?"

Lynette nodded.

"I'm going to give them a call—" He bent to pick up the phone.

"No!" Lynette shouted. She pulled herself off the sofa clumsily. "Ray—"

"Why not?" Ray glared down at his ex-wife. "I should have known. This was just a ploy to get me over here, wasn't it?"

"Ray, please don't be mad. I just thought that once you got here, we could talk."

He was angry now. "Why do you continue to lie and play games?" Shaking his head, Ray said, "Lynn, we have nothing to talk about. Our marriage is over—has been for a long time."

Lynette started to cry. "I l-love you, Ray. I've always loved you. I never lied about that."

Ray moved toward the door. "I have to go."

"Don't walk out on me again. Please, Ray." She reached out to grab his arm.

Pushing her hand away, Ray sighed. "Okay, Lynn. I'll stay for a short while. Say all that you have to say and be done with it." He navigated back over to the recliner and sat down.

Lynn returned to the sofa and sat down, her arms resting over her swollen belly. "I admit I made a lot of mistakes, Ray. But I did what I had to do to keep you."

Ray nodded. "I overlooked a lot of your lies. I kept hoping that you'd finally feel secure—"

"I never felt secure," Lynette interjected. "I never felt loved by you—just contempt. You never forgave me for lying to you about the baby—your baby." Tears rolled down her face. "I needed to feel loved badly and you wouldn't even touch me for months. How do you think you made me feel? That's why I started . . ."

"Having affairs," Ray finished for her. "Lynn, I know that I'm not entirely blameless." He took a deep breath and exhaled slowly before continuing. "I only married you because you threatened to keep what I thought was my unborn child away from me if I didn't. You weren't even pregnant, Lynn. I guess I still resent you for tricking me like that."

"You were going to leave me, Ray. You wanted someone else."

"I loved her."

Lynette lowered her head. "I know."

Ray leaned forward. "We never should have gotten married. Neither one of us was happy. You know it's true."

"All I ever wanted was your love, Ray. Instead, you gave it to some little tramp in the back woods of Georgia . . ." She started to cry once more.

"I never cheated on you after we got married. I was committed to you."

"Except in your heart—that's what I wanted most. I wanted to be the woman in your heart. I wanted a family—"

Ray pointed to her belly. "You will have that now. With your baby's father."

"I wanted a child . . . with you."

He knew from the pain in her eyes that she spoke the truth. Standing up, Ray moved across the room and headed down the short hallway to the bathroom. He returned quickly with a handful of tissues, holding them out to his ex-wife. "I'm sorry, Lynn." Ray eased down beside her.

Lynette pulled herself together. "You know what's funny?" Covering his hand with hers, she said, "I really believe this baby is yours, Ray. There is a chance that it is. What then?"

Ray leaned back and put his hands to his face. "I don't know, Lynn. No matter what you say, I don't believe it's mine. I was gone most of the month that you conceived this child. And when I was home, we fought like cats and dogs."

"Not all of—oooh," Lynette groaned loudly.

He was instantly concerned. "What's wrong?"

"The baby just kicked. It has to be a boy with a kick like that." Smiling, she placed his hand on her stomach.

Ray snatched his hand back when he felt movement. "Don't . . ." He stood up. "I need to go."

Lynette nodded sadly. "Thank you for coming by."

She moved to stand, but Ray stopped her by saying, "Don't get up. I'll lock the door behind me. Turn the alarm on before you go to bed." He stopped at the door. "Take care of yourself and your baby."

The only response was her soft weeping.

CHAPTER 4

"Good morning, Carrie." Stacy, a senior accountant for Steele Accounting Firm, greeted her as she walked through the door. "Did you get settled into your apartment all right?"

"Hello, Stacy. Yes, my son and I are all moved in," Carrie replied smoothly. "We even managed to go shopping for furniture over the weekend."

Stacy offered Carrie a steaming cup of black coffee. "How old is your son? You'll have to add cream and sugar. I didn't know how you take yours."

"Thanks, I just take it like this. Mikey will soon be four." Carrie pulled a picture frame out of a cardboard box. "This is Mikey."

Stacy brushed back her long strawberry-blonde tendrils, leaning over for a better view. "He's so cute. He looks just like you."

Beaming, Carrie acknowledged, "He's my pride and joy."

"I'm so sure. I love kids."

Carrie looked up from putting her things away. "How many do you have?"

Stacy seemed to suddenly become withdrawn. Finally, she said evenly, "I don't have any."

"Oh."

She went on to explain, "I'm one of those women who can't have children. I've done all the right things, but for whatever reason, just can't conceive."

"I'm sorry, Stacy." Carrie could see the shimmer of tears in the woman's sky-blue eyes. "But don't give up hope. Miracles happen every day."

"I haven't." She brushed her hands down her conservative pinstripe pantsuit. Retrieving a tissue from her pocket, Stacy held it up to her nose. "Excuse me, but I'm getting over a cold." She turned away to sneeze. When Stacy turned around, Carrie pretended not to notice her red nose.

Clearing her throat, Stacy then said, "Well, enough about me and my problems. I'm glad you decided to take the job. We've heard very good things about you. After meeting you in person, I can see why Bob's friend thinks so much of you."

"Do you know who this person is?"

"No, not really. Bob says he wishes to remain anonymous."

"Don't you think it's really odd?"

Stacy's blue eyes twinkled. "No, actually I think it's kind of romantic."

Carrie raised her eyebrows. "Romantic?"

"I think the man must be infatuated with you."

"I certainly hope not."

"Why? Are you seeing someone?"

"No. But I'm not interested in a relationship. Not even companionship. I have my son. I don't need anything else right now. I like my life the way it is."

"Oh, that may not be the case at all. I'm simply making an assumption."

Carrie was relieved. "Are those for me?" she asked, pointing to the stack of papers Stacy was holding.

She nodded. "Yes, I almost forgot. Bob wanted me to give these to you. He'll be in around noon today."

"Thanks, Stacy."

"I hope you're not offended by anything I said. I shouldn't have said—"

"It's fine. We were just talking, that's all. Believe me, I've come up with several possible reasons why this person is so interested in me. We won't ever know for sure, but I appreciate his efforts. I really do."

Stacy nodded and smiled. "How about I take you to one of the best restaurants in this city for lunch? It'll be my treat."

Carrie pushed back a curling strand of light-brown hair. Looking down at her navy double-breasted suit, she said, "You don't have to do that." No one in the workplace had ever treated her this kindly before. Even Brandeis had always kept a professional distance when they worked together. "You don't have to buy me lunch, I mean."

"But I want to," Stacy insisted. "I hope we'll become good friends." Stealing a glance at the clock on the wall, Stacy gasped. "Oh my gosh! I'd better go get ready for my nine o'clock appointment. I didn't know it was this late. If you need anything or have any questions, just give me a buzz, okay?"

Carrie nodded. "Thanks, Stacy."

The rest of the day flew by for Carrie. Her first day with Steele Accounting Firm had been a great one. After Stacy's meeting, she'd come back and trained her on posting the accounts payable entries. Carrie learned quickly. She found she truly enjoyed her job.

After a great lunch with Stacy, she'd returned and completed the rest of her tasks alone. After Mikey was born,

Carrie had decided to go back to college. She attended night school, majoring in accounting. She'd received her bachelor's degree almost a year ago. Bob Steele offered as part of her compensation package to pay her tuition, should she decide to pursue furthering her education. Carrie was very tempted, but decided to hold off until Mikey was acclimated to his new environment. It was her goal to become a Certified Public Accountant.

Arriving home, Carrie rushed through the glass doors, yelling, "Hold the elevator, please."

"Thank—" She stopped short. It was Ray. She straightened her five-foot-three petite frame, and turned her back to him.

Biting back a smile, Ray said quietly, "You're quite welcome, Carrie."

She said nothing, and just continued to stand with her back to him. Her heart was racing and it was upsetting. After the way Ray had treated her all those years ago, she couldn't understand why her pulse quickened around him.

"How was your day?"

"Don't talk to me," she snapped, without looking back at him. Although Carrie refused to pay attention to him, she could feel Ray's gaze on her.

"Carrie, if you would let me explain."

She whirled around then to face him. "There's nothing to explain. I was a dumb little country girl who thought the little boy from the big city cared about me. I thought you were a real man. But then I found out just how wrong I was. It's over and done with so there's nothing to talk about."

"I never considered you a dumb country girl. I realize I handled things wrong back then. I would like for us—"

Carrie's head shot up. The look she gave him was filled with raw pain. He knew what she was thinking. Somewhere inside him joy leapt to life. She still cared about him.

"What? Try again?" Carrie shook her head. "I don't think so."

A smile played upon his lips. "I was going to say that maybe we could try being friends. Start over again. Leave the past behind us."

Embarrassed, Carrie ran her hand down the length of her silk jacket. Of course he wouldn't have been talking about them getting back together. He never wanted her in the first place, she painfully acknowledged to herself.

When she glanced up again, she said softly, "It may be that simple for you, but it's not that easy for me, Ray. I'm trying very hard to avoid making the same mistakes over and over again. I don't think being friends is a good idea." The elevator door opened and she rushed off, walking briskly to her apartment. She'd stopped home first to change before heading to Mikey's school. Tonight was open house and Mikey would be waiting.

Everyone had left Steele Accounting Firm, except for two people.

"How did everything go today?"

Bob Steele leaned his slender body back into his chair, eyeing the muscular man standing near the window, looking out. "Everything went well. Carrie's a hard worker. She barely stopped to have lunch."

The light-skinned man turned around slowly, propping his muscular torso against the windowsill. "I hope she and the boy will be very happy here."

"I saw a picture of the little guy. He looks exactly like her. It's almost as if she created him all by herself." Bob raised a glass of bourbon to his lips, the golden amber liquid trickling down his throat.

Head down, his guest nodded slowly. "I guess that's good. She doesn't need to be reminded of all the pain and hurt when she looks him in the face. I'm sure it's hard enough on her having gone through everything that she has.''

Bob sat his brandy snifter down noisily before moving to stand beside his friend at the window. "She's come through it well. I still can't believe all you've told me—''

"That's why I'm doing all this. I have to make it up to her somehow. Carrie didn't deserve to go through such hell! I certainly don't want the boy to suffer." His ice-green eyes flashed in anger. "When I think of what . . .''

Bob laid a hand on his friend's shoulder. "It's in the past.''

"Do you think she'll ever understand? That boy is the only family I have left. I can't just . . .''

Bob shrugged. "I don't know, man. She seems to be a very caring person. After the initial shock wears off, I'm sure she'll understand and not hold it against you.''

Ray resisted the urge to go knocking on Carrie's door. He'd hoped they would be able to at least talk about what happened between them. There was so much he wanted to say to her. But what could he say that would make her understand?

Damn Lynette. If it had not been for her lies, he and Carrie would probably be happily married now. He closed his eyes to the feeling of lonely sadness.

The next day, shortly after Carrie and Mikey arrived home, they heard footsteps outside the door. Mikey jumped up, running toward the door. "I bet that's Ray.''

"Mikey, come back here," Carrie ordered. "Leave that man alone, Honeychile. He probably just wants to be by himself.''

"Ray said I could visit with him anytime I wanted. I want to visit him now.''

Carrie grabbed Mikey by the hand before he could take off like a tornado to the front door. "Oh, no, you don't. Maybe another day, but not tonight, okay?"

Mikey stuck his lips out in a pout. "But why?"

"Because I said so. Dinner will be ready soon and then you've got to have your bath—"

"I won't stay long."

"Mikey, Sweetie, I said no." Her tone was definite and final. "That man worked all day long. I'm sure he's tired. Now, we'll see about another night."

She smiled when her son headed to his room, his little chubby body in a slump. How had Mikey become so attached to Ray? Carrie wondered. How was she going to keep him away from Ray? She had no idea, except that she had to. "I won't let you hurt my son the way you hurt me. I won't."

The weekend was finally here. The bunkbeds for Mikey and a queen-size bed for Carrie arrived. After having them assembled and placed exactly where she wanted them, she and Mikey made them up together. It was a warm August day, so they'd decided to spend the rest of the afternoon in a nearby park. Carrie pushed Mikey back and forth on the swing. His laughter filled the air. Several times the hair on the back of her neck stood up. Carrie surveyed the park, but found nothing out of the ordinary.

"Push, Mommy," Mikey called out.

Carrie's eyes darted around the park. "Huh?"

"Push me."

Carrie forced a smile. "Aren't you tired of the swing yet?"

"No."

"Okay." She pushed him, watching his little legs go up into the air. While listening to the squeal of his laughter, once again she felt that same sensation of being watched.

Her body tensed, as this time it was stronger than the time before. Looking around, she couldn't see anything or anybody. Feeling a thread of fear, she reached out to stop the swing.

"Mommy, why are you stopping?"

Carrie quickly pulled him off the swing. "Mikey, Honey, I think we should leave. Okay?"

"But why?"

"Mommy's not feeling well." Lifting him off the swing, she carried him to the car. Just as she was about to pull out of the parking lot, she noticed a shiny black Corvette. The windows were tinted, but she could still make out the silhouette of someone sitting in the car. Chills spread throughout her body. As if the driver knew he'd been spied, he sped out of the parking lot, leaving a trembling Carrie in his wake.

"You okay, Mommy?"

Carrie nodded and started the car. "I'll be fine once we get home."

In the safe confines of their apartment, Mikey ate his lunch and watched a Disney video. After seeing to her son's comfort, Carrie laid down to take a nap. She fell into troubled sleep. Visions of Martin drifted into the fiery haze of her dreams. Shaking her head, trying to force the terrifying images out of her mind, Carrie tossed fitfully. No matter how hard she tried, she couldn't escape him. He was everywhere—in the Corvette, the car in Georgia. Martin was everywhere, leaving flames in his stead. Carrie screamed.

"Mommy. Mommy, wake up."

Carrie opened her eyes to find Mikey shaking her. Pulling him into her arms, she whispered. "I didn't mean to scare you, Honey. Mommy had a bad dream."

"Don't be skeared, Mommy. I'll take a nap with you." He crawled into her bed and laid next to her, patting her softly on the back. "It's all right now. When you wake up, you'll feel much better, Mommy."

Carrie smiled. "Yes, Baby. It's all right now. You're my brave little man."

Mikey sat up. "Hey, Mommy, can I have a birthday party?"

Carrie massaged her temples before answering. "Sure, do you know who you want to invite?"

"Yeah." He named several children from his new school. "I want Auntie Bran, Uncle Jackson, Ray . . ."

"Er . . . Ray may not be able to come, Honey."

"He said if it was okay with you, he would."

Carrie sat up then. "When did you see Ray?"

"The other day when I was outside. He can come, cain't he?"

Carrie shrugged. "I guess so."

"Mommy, when is my birthday?"

"In two months."

"That's a long time away, Mommy."

"No, it's not. It'll be here before you know it."

Yawning, Mikey laid his head in her lap. "Is, too, a long time. Like Christmas." He yawned again, this time closing his eyes. He soon fell asleep.

Carrie brushed the crumbs off his face as he slept. He looked like a little angel to her. Her heart overflowed from the love her son gave her. To him, she was perfect. He loved her unconditionally. Carrie resolved to give him the mother he deserved. But what if she couldn't? What if she were losing her mind? What kind of mother would she be to him then?

She recalled the panic she'd felt earlier. Would his father forever haunt her?

CHAPTER 5

Carrie's eyes strayed involuntarily to Ray, who was listening as Mikey introduced his best friend, Willie. He seems to really like children, she thought. And they all seemed fascinated by him, as well. Carrie was pleased she'd finally relented and invited him to Mikey's birthday party. She smiled as she recalled his look of disbelief when she'd first approached him.

Ray looked up and caught her watching him. She flushed hotly before heading to the kitchen. He was about to go after her when the doorbell rang. Mikey answered the door and called him back.

"Ray, come here, I want to show you to my godparents."

Two adults and one little boy walked into the apartment.

Grinning, Ray asked, "Are all of them your godparents? Including this young man here?"

Mikey giggled. "Naw. Just Auntie Bran and Uncle Jackson." He pointed to Brian. "This here's my godbrother, Brian."

The exotic-looking woman with hazel eyes spoke up. "Hello, I'm Brandeis, and this is my husband, Jackson."

"It's nice to meet all of you. I'm Ray. I live next door."

"He's going to be my daddy," Mikey announced proudly.

Brandeis and Jackson looked at one another stunned. Finally, Brandeis spoke. "Oh, really?"

Before Ray could respond, he caught sight of Carrie's petite form as she rushed to greet her friends. "Mikey! Stop telling people that," Carrie admonished. "I'm so glad to see all of you. Thank you for coming all this way! And disregard what you heard. It's definitely not true."

Ray moved out of the way as everyone hugged and kissed their greetings. The next person to arrive was Stacy with her nephew in tow.

Later, Brandeis, Carrie, and Stacy sat watching as Ray tumbled around on the floor with Mikey and a couple of his friends. Jackson played Nintendo with Stacy's nephew, and from their vantage point, it looked like Andrew was winning.

"Ray has certainly taken to Mikey, hasn't he?" Brandeis observed.

Carrie followed Brandeis's line of vision. She could tell Ray and the boys were engaged in a bantering sort of conversation. Soon the three boys and Ray were rolling around on the floor in front of the television. She turned away. "Humph."

Brandeis and Stacy exchanged quizzical glances.

"What's that supposed to mean?" Stacy asked.

"Nothing," Carrie muttered.

When Carrie said nothing more, Brandeis posed a question of her own. "Why don't you tell me what's going on between you and Ray?"

"There's nothing going on between us."

Brandeis downed the last of her soda before responding. "I see."

Carrie caught the exchange of knowing smiles between the two women. "Really. There's nothing going on."

"We believe you," they both chorused, but it was as clear as day that they didn't.

Carrie got up off the sofa and walked off in a huff.

Lowering her voice and leaning toward Brandeis, Stacy whispered, "Looks like Carrie is fighting her attraction to Ray. I wonder for how long, though. He seems like such a nice guy. And it's obvious he cares for her and Mikey. He can barely keep his eyes off her."

"Carrie's been through a lot. I think she's just being cautious."

Stacy nodded her head sympathetically. "I can certainly understand that. I've certainly had my share of bad relationships." Hearing Carrie come out of the kitchen, she glanced around. "Oh, Carrie just brought out the cake and ice cream. I think I'll go help her cut the cake."

"Stacy, you're going to sneak a piece. I see that gleam in your eye," Brandeis teased.

Putting a finger to her mouth, Stacy said, "Shhh. Don't tell everybody."

"Where's Stacy off to in such a hurry?" Jackson settled back on the sofa and put his arms around his wife. He placed a gentle kiss on her cheek.

"She's going to get cake and ice cream."

"Mikey seems to be enjoying his birthday party. Looks like he's gotten taller since we last saw him."

"Yes, he does. He's growing so fast."

"Does Mikey remind you of Martin?" Jackson asked.

Nodding, Brandeis said, "Yes, at times, but he reminds me of the goodness in Martin."

Jackson pulled her deeper into the fold of his arm. "Have I told you lately how much I love you?"

"No, not lately."

Lowering his voice, he murmured huskily, "I love you, Bran."

"I love you, Jackson."

Carrie walked up behind the two. "You two lovebirds

are getting on my last nerve! Stop all that smooching while I round up the boys.''

Laughing, Jackson stood up. "Why don't you go on over there and spend some time with Ray. I'll round up the boys. That poor man has been watching you all afternoon and you haven't given him the time of day.''

"Jackson, he's Mikey's friend, not mine. Let Mikey entertain him." Carrie stormed off.

Looking at his wife, Jackson asked, "What's going on between the two of them? Carrie acts as if she hates the man. And she's using that kitchen as a refuge.''

"I know. It doesn't make sense. If I disliked someone, I sure wouldn't let him around my son.''

"Honey, I'm going to go over and have a talk with Ray. Maybe we can get some answers from him. Carrie sure isn't talking.''

Jackson made his way over to where Ray was standing. "I noticed you and Carrie barely said two words to each other. Is something going on between you two?''

Ray shook his head. "Nothing's going on, Jackson. Carrie and I have a history together. I hurt her and she's never forgiven me. It's as simple as that. If it wasn't for Mikey, she'd make sure I wasn't anywhere near her.''

"Oh.''

"Why are you so concerned?''

Jackson pushed his glasses up. "Because she is a close friend of the family. She's been through a lot, and my wife and I don't want to see her get hurt again." His tone held the trace of a warning.

"I don't want to hurt her, Jackson. I never wanted to hurt her. I care a great deal for her.''

Jackson believed him. "Do you mind telling me what happened?''

Ray shook his head. "I don't mind." He related the

events of what happened during his time in Georgia, his marriage, and eventual divorce. When he was done, Jackson let out a soft whistle.

"Man, I wish you luck," Jackson said, before joining his wife.

Ray nodded. "I'm going to need it," he whispered to himself.

Later that evening, Ray lounged on his leather sofa, a glass of cognac in his hand. An image of Carrie flashed across his mind as he sipped the warm liquor. He had hoped to learn from Jackson more of what had happened to Carrie after he'd left Georgia, but he never got the chance. He was partly relieved that he hadn't been the total reason she had built this wall around herself. Yet it angered him that someone else had hurt her so deeply. Would she ever recover?

As much as he wanted to stay around long enough to speak with Carrie alone, Ray decided to leave early. He wanted to give her time with Jackson and Brandeis since they'd come all the way from Virginia to visit her and Mikey for the weekend.

Ray's thoughts were interrupted by the ringing doorbell. "This had better not be you, Lynn." Ever since that night they'd had that talk, she constantly called. A few times, she'd tried to invite herself over. Ray wouldn't put it past her to just show up. Grumbling, he raised himself up and headed to the door. Standing before him was a young woman grinning from ear to ear.

"Kaitlin, it's good to see you. Come on in."

Strolling in with her hands on her hips, the tall, slender woman whirled on him. "What's up, Ray? You're too busy to call anyone?"

He backed away, laughing. "Hey, calm down. I tried to call you last night."

"Yeah, right. I can't believe you're tripping like this."

"I'm not tripping, Kaitlin. I'm a working man, or have you forgotten?"

"Oh, so it's your job that's been keeping you busy? That's what you're trying to say? I've been home for a week and haven't heard from you."

Ray settled back onto the sofa. "Girl, what's wrong with you? Did you have a bad day today at one of your stores?"

"No, I didn't have a bad day. Lynn's been calling to inform me, and anybody else that'll listen, that the two of you are getting back together. When in hell did that happen?"

He sat up straight. "She said what?"

"You heard me." Kaitlin rolled her dark eyes, then strolled over to a nearby mirror, fingering through her short hairstyle.

Ray shook his head in denial. "I'm sure I couldn't have heard you correctly."

She nodded. "You heard me. Lynn told me that the two of you are getting back together. She also called Jillian and Ivy. I wouldn't put it past her to have called everyone in our entire family."

"And you believed her?"

"I don't know what to believe." Kaitlin plopped down on the burgundy leather loveseat.

"You must think I'm crazy."

"No, Ray, I don't. I just hope you know what you're doing. But I'll tell you this. Jillian says that Mama is so upset right now, she's spitting nails. You know Lynn called her, too."

Ray put his hands to his face. "I can't believe this. The woman is crazy. We are not getting back together. She had me come over one night on a goose chase and we talked. I mean really talked, but that was all." Ray shook his head, his mind reeling from all Kaitlin told him. "What is her problem?"

Kaitlin sighed. "I'm so glad you're not getting back with her. You're my brother and I want you to be happy, but I don't see it happening with Lynn. She's too manipulative. Always been that way. She treats you like a puppet on a string—a string of lies."

"Believe me, Sis, I know Lynn is a big liar. You can't believe anything that comes out of her mouth . . . Jesus, now I'll have to call Mama and listen to her rant and rave."

"And I don't think I'm going to hang around for that. It's going to be ugly. But hey, after Mama gets through chewing you out, I'm thinking about catching a movie. Want to come?" She rose to stand. "I really just stopped by to see if you were still breathing."

"You're turning into a liar like Lynn. You came by to see if she was here with me." Ray shook his head, "You should know me better than that. As far as the movie goes—not tonight. I'm tired, so I think I'll just go to bed early. This past week has been hell on me."

Kaitlin made a face. "I sure don't envy you, Deputy U.S. Marshal. I wouldn't have your job for nothing." She picked up her purse and placed it across her shoulder. "Walk me to my place, big brother. I have something for you upstairs in my apartment. I found it on this last buying trip."

Ray stood up. "I can't believe that woman."

"Don't trip off it. She'll get hers. You'll see." Kaitlin grabbed Ray by the arm. "Come on and forget about her. Walk me upstairs."

Mikey had found a friend and a playmate in Ray. And herself? A heart full of pain, that's what he had brought her. Ray and Martin were both painful reminders of some of the biggest mistakes she'd ever made. Many years had passed since her break-up with Ray, and still, each time he looked at her, Carrie felt the exhilaration of his sensual eyes as they caressed her face and lingered on her lips.

He'd left her empty of everything except despair—despair that had gradually turned to hate. At least she had convinced herself it was hate, until she saw him again. Now Carrie didn't know what she felt for him.

Carrie gathered up all of the colorful gift wrapping, plates, and cups, and tossed them in a huge plastic bag. "I'm taking the trash out, Sweetie."

Without taking his eyes off the television, Mikey responded, "Okay, Mommy."

She opened her door and walked briskly down to the trash incinerator. As she headed back up the hallway to her apartment, she heard Ray's door open. Carrie was about to speak until she realized he was not alone. A tall, slender woman with short, bouncy curls, flawless skin that was the color of dark chocolate, and a mole just above her lip, under her left nostril, stood beside him.

Carrie subconsciously brushed her own warm brown errant curls away from her face. Holding her head down, she intended to walk past them without speaking. To her dismay, Ray stopped in front of her.

"Hello, Carrie. I want you to meet someone."

Refusing to look at them, she managed to say, "I don't have time right now; I left Mikey alone." She stepped around Ray, not once acknowledging his friend.

"Carrie—"

She kept walking, pretending that she hadn't heard him call her name. She could still hear them talking.

"What's wrong with her?"

Ray shrugged. "I have no idea."

Back in her apartment, Carrie started dinner. As she cooked, she fumed. Oh, that dog! Ray hadn't changed a bit. And then he had the nerve to try to flaunt his girlfriend in her face. Assuming he was only walking her to the elevator, she headed to the door with the intention of confronting him. Carrie waited with her back pressed against the door. When minutes passed and he hadn't returned, she started back to the kitchen.

Carrie held her breath as she heard the familiar jingle of Ray's keys as he passed by. When she heard his door open and close, Carrie exhaled. She decided confronting him might not be such a good idea. It would only serve to make him think she was jealous. And she wasn't. Carrie started at the sound of someone knocking on her door. She was only mildly surprised to find Ray standing there.

"What do you want?" she snapped.

Ray scratched his head. "It's funny. I don't remember you ever being this rude."

"I'm sure there's a lot you don't remember about me."

"On the contrary. There's a lot I remember vividly."

Carrie warmed under his intense scrutiny. "I've got to go."

When she tried to move away, he grasped her arm. "Wait, Carrie. All I wanted to do was introduce you to Kaitlin."

"Why on earth would I want to meet her? You know what? I'm really sick of you forcing yourself into my life. Mikey may like being around you, but I don't. You have the nerve of a billygoat, thinking I would want to meet your current fool."

Carrie could see the sparks of anger igniting in the depths of his dark-brown eyes. He expelled his breath in a half-angry sigh, before saying, "Kaitlin is far from being a fool. She has known me longer than any—"

"She's a fool as far as I'm concerned. And I don't care how long she's known you. Anybody who gets involved with you is a fool."

Ray was clearly offended. "How long are you going to be unreasonable like this?" He sighed in resignation. "I don't need your insults, Carrie. I was trying to be nice. Your son and I enjoy each other's company, but if you don't want me around, I'll stay away from the both of you."

"Suits me." She slammed the door in his face. Carrie

felt a deep sense of disappointment settle over her after her confrontation with Ray. The nerve of that man. What did he expect her to do after he flaunted his girlfriend in her face? She'd learned from Mikey that he was recently divorced. He certainly hadn't wasted any time in finding a replacement. Carrie silently refused to acknowledge how much this bothered her.

Calling to mind his hurt expression, Carrie felt guilty over her treatment of Ray. Mikey was going to be crushed. Maybe she shouldn't have slammed the door on Ray and his relationship with her son. With Mikey, he was warm, caring, and funny. It was strangely comforting somehow to see the two of them together. And that's what scared her, Carrie admitted silently.

Why was she so afraid of Ray? Because she realized that falling for him again wouldn't be difficult. He was many of the things she'd always wanted in a man. And a few of the things she didn't want. Carrie could not afford to open her heart up for more pain. Mikey needed her. But more than that, she needed herself. Love had almost destroyed her twice. She vowed there wouldn't be a third time. No matter what her feelings for Ray were.

CHAPTER 6

When Ray opened the door, he half expected it to be Carrie. As Kaitlin breezed in by him, he asked, "Didn't I just walk you upstairs to your place?"

"Yeah, but silly me, I left my jacket down here, so I came back to get it."

Following her, Ray shook his head. "Girl, you are so forgetful. If your head weren't attached to your body . . ."

Kaitlin waved him off with her hand. "Sooo, what happened with little Miss Attitude next door after I left? Who is she, anyway?"

Ray's eyes sparkled with laughter. "That's the real reason for your return visit. You're not fooling anyone."

"Humph. I could have called and asked." She leaned against the wet bar. "Now come on, what did you do to piss her off so quick? I know she hasn't been living here that long." Following Ray into his living room, she sat down on the arm of the loveseat. "Matter of fact, I didn't know anyone had moved in."

Ray sat down and settled back into the deep leather

cushions. "I met her years ago in Georgia. Her name is Carrie."

Kaitlin's eyes grew wide with surprise. "She's the one—"

His mouth went grim. "Only now she hates me with a passion."

"Then she must still care for you, or she wouldn't be that mad."

His eyebrows shot up in surprise and he asked, "You really think so? From where I'm sitting, it looks like the woman really despises me. Matter of fact, I told her tonight that I'd planned to stay as far away from her as possible."

Kaitlin shook her head. "I wouldn't do that, Ray. You've got to win back her trust. She feels used—I can't say I blame her. If it had been me—you'd be dead . . . with that group of overprotective brothers that I have. Not to mention overbearing—"

Ray laughed. "Okay already. I get the point."

"Well, I guess I'd better get to know her." Throwing her jacket over her shoulder, she stood up and walked over to Ray. Bending, she planted a kiss on her brother's cheek. "Well, goodnight a second time, big brother. I'll talk to you later."

He sat forward and looked at her intently. "You sure you have all of your belongings this time?" Ray asked before cracking a smile.

Rolling her eyes, she responded, "I think so." Kaitlin moved across the room in quick feminine strides.

"Call me when you get home," Ray ordered before standing up.

Kaitlin laughed. "Yes, father. I'll call you."

"Smartass," he murmured, while holding the door open for her.

He could hear his sister's laughter as she headed to the elevators. Standing outside his apartment, Ray listened for the dinging sound that would announce the elevator's arrival. When he felt sure Kaitlin was safely en route to her place, Ray entered his apartment and locked up for the night.

Carrie crossed his mind, causing him to flinch in anger. She'd had no reason to be so damn rude. Things between them were getting out of hand. This was not the way Ray wanted it, and he didn't want to hurt Mikey because of Carrie's attitude toward him. He genuinely cared for the little boy.

Ray changed his mind about going straight to bed and decided to make another attempt to talk to Carrie. He left his apartment and knocked on her door. He was surprised to see Mikey answering the door. "What are you still doing up, little man?"

"Mommy said I could stay up for a little while longer since it's my birthday."

Ray kneeled to Mikey's eye level. "You've got to be more careful when answering the door. Remember what I told you?"

Staring down at the floor, Mikey nodded. "I forgot, Ray. I'm sorry."

"I'll tell you what. I'm going to go back outside and close the door. Let's start over."

"Okay, Ray. I'll remember. You'll see." He looked up at him with those adoring eyes and Ray couldn't resist hugging his little chubby body before standing up.

After closing the door, Ray waited a few minutes before ringing the doorbell.

"Yes, who's here?" Mikey's scratchy voice could be heard through the door.

Biting back laughter, Ray responded, "It's me, Ray."

Mikey opened the door grinning. "See. I did real good, didn't I?"

Ray ran his fingers through Mikey's hair. "You sure did, Son. You did just fine. But you have to remember to keep it up." He glanced around the room. "Where is your mother?"

"She's taking a shower. She likes to do that a lot. She takes a long time, too."

"Well, I'm not going to stay. I want you and your mom to meet my sister, Kaitlin. She lives on the tenth floor of this building."

Mikey grabbed Ray by the hand. "I don't want you to leave. You can stay and read me a story."

Ray shook his head. "It's kind of late, but if you're good, I'll do it another night. Real soon."

"You won't forget, will you?"

Picking up the small child, Ray carried him to the door. "I won't forget, little man. Now I want you to take care of your mother for me."

"I will."

Ray put Mikey down. "Don't forget to lock the door behind me."

"I'll lock the door. Bye, Ray."

"Goodnight, Son." He made his way back to his apartment. Carrie had an adorable little boy. Ray wished selfishly that Mikey had been the result of his brief union with Carrie. If she had been pregnant, he would have married her immediately. But instead, Lynette had been the one claiming to be pregnant. As much as he loved Carrie, he left her because he had a responsibility to his child. A child that hadn't existed.

When Carrie stepped out of the shower, she heard Mikey laughing and talking to someone. Carrie hurried into a pair of sweats and rushed out. Mikey was alone on the sofa watching TV. "Who in the world were you talking to?"

"Ray."

Her eyes opened up and her mouth parted. Ray had come back here? "Honey, I've told you not to go around answering the door unless I specifically tell you to do so."

"I opened the door but Ray made me close it and do

it again. I didn't open it until I knowed it was Ray. He told me to never open the door unless I knowed who it was."

"Until you knew who it was."

"Huh?"

A smile played at the edge of Carrie's mouth. "Never mind, Sweetie. What did Ray want?" She couldn't believe he'd come back after the things they'd said to each other.

"He wanted us to meet his sister, Kaitlin. I told him you was taking a shower. And that you take them for a real long time."

That's just great, she thought. "I'm sure he didn't need to know that."

Mikey shrugged. "He asked me what you was doing. His sister lives here in the building with us."

Carrie's mind was somewhere else. His sister. The tall beautiful woman was his sister. There had been a striking resemblance between them. She'd been too stunned to notice it earlier. Carrie smiled widely before she caught herself. Why was she so delighted?

Thinking about Ray, and the way she reacted over the weekend, had Carrie praying that she wouldn't run into him when she arrived home. She peered into her rear view mirror intending to change lanes, when she glimpsed a dark Corvette, partially hidden behind the burgundy Cadillac following her. Carrie made a left turn at the first light she came to, and so did the Corvette. Nervous, she drove past her apartment building, hoping her suspicions were wrong.

"Mommy, we passed our building. Where're we going?"

"Nowhere, Baby. Mommy's just thinking about something and drove too fast to turn into the garage," she lied. Carrie didn't want to scare Mikey. When the Corvette seemed to continue following her, she made one last turn before heading back to the building.

As she turned to enter the garage, Carrie released a long sigh when the car kept going. Not once did it slow down. She couldn't clearly make out the driver because of the dark windows. With her heart pounding loudly in her ears, she and Mikey walked briskly into the lobby. While they waited for the elevator, Carrie checked her mailbox. Feeling the hairs on her neck standing up, she took a peek outside. The gleaming black Corvette was now parked across the street.

"Mommy, the elevator's here," Mikey called.

"I-I'll be right there." Carrie's fingers shook nervously as she scanned the envelopes in her hand. She jumped when the doors opened on her floor. Ray was standing there.

"I didn't mean to scare you."

Carrie was on the verge of tears, but she murmured, "I-I'm okay."

Ray seemed to sense her distress. Placing a comforting hand on her petite shoulder, he asked, "Carrie? Is something wrong?"

"Why do you ask?"

He lowered his voice. "I can't believe I scared you that much. You seem kind of jumpy. As if you've seen a ghost. You know you can talk to me about anything."

As she tried to keep her fragile control, Carrie knew she couldn't continue to live in fear. Someone had been watching her house in Georgia. Now, that someone was here in California.

"Carrie?" Ray prompted.

Snapping out of her reverie, she said, "Actually, Ray, do you have a few minutes? I do need to talk to someone."

Nodding toward her son, he asked, "Do you want to wait until you have Mikey settled?"

Mikey stood a few feet away from them, making faces in the mirror. Carrie took a deep breath and tried to relax. "No, I'd rather talk now. Do you have a few minutes?"

"I have some time."

Together they headed down the hallway.

When they were seated in her apartment, Carrie sent Mikey to take his bath, but not before Mikey called out to Ray.

"What is it, little man?"

"Please don't leave before I'm done with my bath."

"I won't."

Awkwardly, Carrie cleared her throat. "Ray. . . I know this might sound a little crazy to you, but somebody has been following me. At first I thought it was just my imagination, but it's not."

"Do you have any idea why someone would be following you or who it might be?"

How could she tell him she thought it was a dead man? Carrie shook her head. "No, I don't."

"What about an old boyfriend? Have you been threatened or anything?"

Carrie shook her head again. "I haven't dated anyone in a while."

"When did you notice that you were being followed?"

"Before I left Georgia. One night Mikey woke me up and I couldn't go back to sleep. I happened to look out of my window and there was a black Corvette parked near the house. There was a man sitting in it . . . watching my house."

"Did you call the police?"

"No, at the time, I thought maybe I'd imagined it. I left the window and a few minutes later, I went back to take another look. The car was gone. I hadn't seen it again until I moved out here. Since I've been in California, I've seen that same car a few times. Including tonight."

"Are you sure it's the exact same car? There are—"

She pursed her lips into a displeasing line. "I know there are lots of Corvettes, but I'm pretty sure it's the same car. You know how you drive your green Lexus—well, you would know your car anywhere. No matter how many you see, you will know your car. It's the same with this Corvette. I know it's the same car."

"Did you happen to see the license plate?"

She stared fixedly. "Well, no. I wasn't really looking for it either."

"Next time you see this car, try to get the license number."

"Okay." She felt so silly for not thinking of that on her own.

"When you pulled into the garage, was the car still following you?"

Carrie nodded. "Yes. It would never get too close, so I didn't get a glimpse of the driver, but I think it's a man. Anyway, he kept going when I pulled into the garage. But while Mikey and I waited for the elevator, I checked my mail and happened to peek outside—the car was parked across the street."

Ray stood up quickly. "I'm going downstairs to check if it's still there. I'll be right back."

Carrie followed him to the door. He had been gone mere seconds when Mikey came running into the living room half wearing, half dragging a towel with a basketball theme.

"Where's Ray, Mommy?"

"He'll be right back, Sweetie. He's had to check on something." Grabbing Mikey by the hand, she led him to his bedroom. "Let's find you something to put on before Ray gets back. We don't want to shock him by you running around naked all over the apartment."

Mikey giggled.

Carrie had Mikey dressed by the time Ray knocked on the door and called out, "It's Ray, Carrie."

She rushed to let him in. "Was it still there?"

He shook his head. "No, I didn't see anything."

Carrie's shoulders slumped. "I just wish this weren't

happening to me. I don't want to live my life in fear," she stated in a low, tormented voice.

"I won't let anything happen to you."

"Ray, can you stay and watch TV with me?" Mikey asked from his position on the couch.

Ray looked down at her. Carrie knew he was silently asking for her permission. She smiled and nodded. "I'd like that, too."

While she cooked, Ray and Mikey sat on the couch watching sitcom after sitcom. She watched them together—like father and son. Mikey was so happy around Ray. So much so, it caused her eyes to fill with tears. Biting her trembling bottom lip, Carrie wished for the first time in a long time that things had worked out for her and Ray. How she had loved him . . . she shook her head, not wanting to think back to that time in her life.

"Carrie?"

She found Ray watching her. "Yes, do you need something?"

"You okay?"

Putting on a bright smile, Carrie nodded. "Would . . . would you like to have dinner with us? It's not much—"

"I'd love to eat with you and little man, here."

Carrie turned away, chastising herself for inviting him to dinner. She was letting Mikey's affection for Ray weaken her determination to avoid men—more specifically, Ray. He'd broken her heart once. She couldn't let him do it again.

"Dinner's ready," Carrie called out thirty minutes later. She'd put together a simple fare of garlic chicken with pasta, steamed vegetables, and muffins.

Mikey said a quick prayer of thanks before they all hungrily attacked their plates.

Mikey put down his fork. "Ray, can I ask you a question?"

"Sure. What do you want to know?"

"Do you shoot people with your gun? Mommy says I

can't have a toy one 'cause guns are bad. She says that people who shoot other people are bad. Are you a bad man?"

Carrie almost choked on her water. "M-Mikey!"

Ray placed a hand over hers. "It's okay." He wiped his mouth and addressed Mikey. "I want to tell you something. If I didn't have to carry a gun, I wouldn't. I'm not crazy about them myself. However, guns are not bad—it's the people that sometimes use them who are bad. So, in a way, your mother is right."

Carrie glanced over at her son. Mikey appeared to be thinking about what Ray was saying. "I'm sorry I confused you, Sweetie. What I should have said is that the person who carries a gun also carries a tremendous amount of responsibility. Just like you are responsible for what happens in your room, that person is responsible for what happens with that gun."

"If you shoot somebody, then it's not the gun's fault—it's the person that held the gun," Mikey stated. "Like when my clothes and toys are on the floor—my room gets dirty and it's my fault cause I don't pick them up, right?"

Ray smiled. "I wear a gun not just to shoot people, but to protect myself and others." Ray leaned closer to the table. "I'll tell you a secret, though. If I had to shoot someone, it wouldn't make me feel good about it at all."

Mikey frowned. "But why? You're the good one."

"That may be true, Mikey, but if I take his life, that's something I can never give back. Death is permanent. Understand?"

Stuffing a forkful of meat into his mouth, Mikey nodded.

"Slow down, Sweetie Pie. The food's not going anywhere," Carrie said, while cutting her meat into bite-size portions. "You'll make yourself sick."

She was thrilled when Ray wanted seconds.

"You've turned out to be a good cook, Carrie. Much better than when I first met you."

Carrie laughed and pointed her fork toward him. "You have no manners whatsoever. I know I was terrible back then, but I ended up taking a cooking class."

"A cooking class? Why? Your mom's a great cook. I still think about her sweet potato pies."

Her laughter bubbled out. "Mama tried to help me, but we only ended up arguing."

Ray joined in her laughter. "Do you remember when you tried to make . . . what was it?"

"It was lasagna. I make a mean lasagna now. Don't I, Mikey?"

"She sure does. She's the bestest cook in the world."

"So there!" Carrie announced.

"I stand corrected," Ray responded. "I haven't seen you smile this much since you moved in. It's refreshing."

Carrie pointed to his plate. "Your food's getting cold, Ray." When he looked at her, gazing deep into her eyes, it made her extremely uncomfortable. It was as if he were searching for truths—truths she preferred to keep hidden.

Ray and Carrie finished dinner as they listened to Mikey talk about his activities at preschool.

Carrie cleared the dishes away and headed to the kitchen.

"I'll help you," Ray offered. His gaze traveled over her face and searched her eyes.

Carrie had to fight her overwhelming need to be close to him again. The sensual scent of his cologne was intoxicating. She inhaled deeply. When she sensed he was still watching her, Carrie flushed and turned away. "You don't have to do that, Ray. Why don't you and Mikey watch TV?"

"Because I think we need to talk. We can talk while I help you clean the kitchen."

"Sure." She was acutely aware of Ray following behind her as she headed into the kitchen.

While she ran her dishwater, Carrie murmured, "Thanks

so much, Ray. I also want to apologize for the way I've been acting. I'm sorry about the other night—''

He waved off her explanation. ''It's forgotten.''

''I didn't know she was your sister.''

Ray laughed. ''Most people say we look a lot alike. I'm surprised you couldn't tell.''

''The only thing I saw was her gender.''

Ray put down the towel he'd been holding and moved to stand beside Carrie. Turning her to face him, he asked, ''It bothered you to think that she and I were involved, didn't it?''

Carrie shook her head and looked away, unable to verbally deny the truth.

''I think you're lying to me. It bothered you. I could see it on your face. You were about to speak until you saw Kaitlin.''

She didn't respond.

''I have four other sisters. They visit me also. I hope we're not going to have to go through this with them.''

''I'm really sorry, Ray. I just thought you were trying to flaunt your girlfriend in my face.''

''I thought you knew me better than that.''

''I thought . . .'' Carrie shook her head, shrugging. ''It doesn't matter.''

''Carrie, I'm not seeing anyone. The only women you'll ever see leaving my house are my five sisters.''

''What about your ex-wife?'' Carrie wanted to know. ''Does she visit you, too?''

''No. She's never been in my apartment, but not for lack of trying on her part. I hope I continue to be this lucky.''

''That's not a very nice thing to say.''

''I know. But it's the way I feel.''

The kitchen clean and tidy, Carrie and Ray returned to the living room and joined Mikey on the sofa.

When Carrie caught her son yawning and struggling to

stay awake, she suggested, "Sweetie, you're tired. Why don't you go to bed?"

"I don't want to go to bed."

Ray offered, "How about if I tell you a story? Will you be a good boy for your mother?"

"Yes, Ray. I'll be a good boy."

He stood and pulled Mikey into his arms. "Come on, little man. Let's go have story time."

Carrie watched as Ray carried her son into his room. Her heart once again filled with sadness over having to raise Mikey alone. Children needed both a mother and a father. The raw ache in her heart spread thoughout her body as she heard the sound of their laughter coming from Mikey's room.

Half an hour later, Ray crept out of Mikey's room. Carrie crawled off the sofa and asked in a loud whisper, "Is he sleeping?"

Ray smiled and nodded. "He went to sleep as soon as I started my story—I wonder if I should be offended?"

Carrie put her hand over her mouth to avoid laughing out loud.

"What's so funny?"

"Nothing. I just think your stories are too drawn out, that's all. At least, that's the way I remember them."

Ray inclined his head and fingered his mustache. "Oh really? I remember you used to love my stories."

"It's not a bad thing," Carrie added quickly. "I think your stories are nice."

"My nieces and nephews have said the same thing." He glanced down at her, searching her face. Carrie wondered what he hoped to find. Before she realized what was happening, Ray leaned over and brushed his lips gently against hers. She held her breath as his tongue met hers.

Ray's kiss sent the pit of her stomach into a wild swirl. Shocked at her own eager response, Carrie pulled away abruptly.

Unable to meet his questioning gaze, she checked her watch. "I guess I'd better get an early start on tomorrow myself."

Ray stood up and straightened his tall frame. "Me, too."

Walking him to the door, Carrie placed a hand on his arm, causing him to pause midstride. "Thanks again, Ray."

"Don't forget, I'm right next door. Just call me if you need me. Mikey has my number." Ray opened the door. "Don't forget to lock up nice and tight after I leave."

"I won't forget," Carrie murmured. And I can't forget that my first love lives right next door, she thought.

"Man, why are you stalking the poor woman? You're going to scare her half to death," Bob admonished.

"I'm not trying to scare her. I wish I could just go up to her and Mikey, instead of doing it this way. I hate this."

"We'll find a way—but you've got to stop following her. One day, she's going to call the cops. I don't think you want that to happen."

"No, I don't, but I don't want to miss out on being a part of Mikey's life either. He's all I have left."

"I understand, but we agreed that Carrie couldn't handle the shock of seeing you right now," Bob argued.

"I know. . . . Maybe we're wrong. Maybe . . ." His ice-green eyes flashed in confusion. "There must be another way. An easier way."

Bob Steele shook his head. "I really think we should keep to our original plan. You can't move too fast on this."

He sighed heavily. "You're probably right, Bob. I don't want to cause them any more pain than they have already endured."

"So, will you please stop following them? If you want to help Carrie, it's best not to scare her."

"You're right. I'm getting impatient. I want to get to know Mikey . . ."

"Give it more time. As we agreed, okay?"

The green-eyed man nodded. "But no matter how she may feel about me, I won't let her keep Mikey away from me."

CHAPTER 7

Mikey struggled to keep up with Carrie as she hauled the basket of freshly laundered clothing in her arms from the laundry room. When they arrived at their apartment, Carrie dropped the basket to the floor. She quickly unlocked her door.

As she opened her door, she heard the sound of Ray's opening.

He stuck his head out. "Carrie, my family's going to Disneyland on Saturday. My sisters and my brothers are taking their kids. Why don't you and Mikey go with me?" Ray winked at Mikey. "I think I wouldn't feel so out of place if I have you with me."

During the exchange, Mikey had maneuvered himself over to Ray's apartment. When Ray stepped into the hallway, Mikey snaked out a small hand and grabbed hold of Ray's little finger. When Ray looked down, it was into a pair of worshipful medium brown eyes.

"Boy, oh, boy. Can we, Mommy, huh?"

Carrie was surprised, to say the least. She certainly

hadn't expected him to do something like this. "Ray, you don't—"

"Carrie, I want to do this. My whole family's going. I'd really like for you and Mikey to come with me. I hate going to places like that alone."

"You won't be alone. You just said your whole family will be there. Mikey and I aren't—"

"Come on, Mommy. Can we, Mommy, huh?"

"Mikey, Honey—"

"Pleeease?"

While Mikey begged, Ray watched Carrie waver. He held his tongue, and finally the boy's enthusiasm won over his mother's better judgment.

"Yes. Yes, you can go to Disneyland with Ray. Now why don't we discuss this further in my apartment?"

"Yeepee. Yeepee. I'm going to Disneyland."

As Mikey danced around the living room, Carrie whispered, "I think that was low what you did. You got what you wanted, so I hope you're satisfied."

"I'd be satisfied if you'd come with us. The invitation included you both."

Carrie shook her head. "I don't think that would be a good idea."

"Why?"

"Mikey, why don't you be a sweetie and go wash your hands?" When Mikey left the room, Carrie turned to Ray, saying, "I don't want to give Mikey the wrong idea. For some reason, he's really stuck on you being his daddy."

Ray looked offended. "You make it sound as if it would be a terrible thing."

"I just meant that I don't want my son getting false hope. I really do appreciate the time you spend with him. He really needs a male figure in his life."

"I'm very fond of him, Carrie."

"Well, now that you've started this, I truly hope this is

not just a passing interest on your part, Ray. Mikey would be so crushed.''

"I wouldn't do that to him."

"I hope not. I'll make you regret the day you ever met me if you hurt my son. I mean it, Ray."

"I would never deliberately hurt either one of you. Now that we've got that settled, will you please accompany me to Disneyland?"

"I don't know. I mean, your family—"

"My family will be delighted to have you join us."

She looked at him with her question in her eyes. "Are you sure about this, Ray?"

"I've never been more sure about anything in my life."

"If you say so." Inwardly, she wondered why he wanted her and Mikey to go with him on what clearly was a family outing.

"Well, that's all I wanted. I know you need to see to the little man. I'll check in with you later this week."

"Thank you for inviting us, Ray. It's really very sweet."

"I think the two of you need some Disney magic right about now."

"We're okay. I've never seen Mikey so happy—I owe it all to you."

"What can I do to make his mother happy?"

Her face clouded with uneasiness. "I . . . I'm fine. There's no need to worry about me."

"I guess I'll have to take your word for it. I'll see you later, Carrie." Ray closed the door and was gone. Inside her apartment, the cool, dark interior offered no welcome. Seeing Ray always disturbed her.

After settling Mikey down for a long afternoon nap, she tried watching television but wasn't really interested in anything on.

Confused over her conflicting feelings, Carrie strolled over to the sliding glass doors. Opening them, she stood on the balcony overlooking the pool area, enjoying the gentle breeze of the afternoon air. It was a beautiful September day. Back in Georgia, the air would be kind of chilly. Carrie marveled over how warm the weather was. She and Mikey were still able to wear their summer shorts.

Disneyland with Ray and his family. Why had she agreed to go? What would his family think? Carrie stretched and yawned. "Oh well, I've already agreed and Mikey's so excited . . ."

Heading back into her apartment, Carrie collapsed onto the sofa, stretching out. Raising herself on one elbow, she tried once more to watch TV.

Each time Ray crept into her mind, she forced him out. "I can't do this, Ray. I can't let you get to me again," she whispered to the empty room.

Ray wasn't sure whether or not he'd made progress with Carrie. He knew she still didn't trust him because she continued to appear guarded around him. "At least she's going to Disneyland with us this weekend." Ray grinned. All Carrie ever talked about was having a close family. He hoped being with him and his family would bring them closer.

Stomach growling, Ray headed to the kitchen in search of nourishment. The doorbell rang. He knew Kaitlin was visiting one of her stores in northern California, and the rest of his family usually called before dropping by. Ray was sure it was Carrie.

"I hope you're not here to tell me you . . ." It wasn't Carrie. "What do you want, Lynette?"

"Hello to you, too. I was in the neighborhood and thought I'd come by to see you. I went to the doctor today and I have sonogram pictures of the baby."

"I hope everything's okay with you and your baby."

"Aren't you going to invite me in, or is this the way you treat pregnant women?"

"Come in." He held the door open. "Is there a reason for this visit?"

Lynette took a tour of the place. "Nice place you have here. It just needs a woman's touch."

"It suits me."

She continued on as if she hadn't heard him. "I would be glad to help you decorate."

"I'm happy with the way it is. If I decide it needs a woman's touch, I'll have my mother or one of my sisters give me a hand."

Lynette bit back a retort.

Ray ran his hand over his face. "I'm tired, Lynn. Why are you here?"

"Because . . . because I miss you, Ray. I haven't heard from you in a while. I thought after our talk that things would be different. I want us to start over—"

"Start over? You've got to be kidding!"

"Please don't be that way, Ray."

Ray shook his head. "Lynn, there's not going to be any starting over. And please stop lying to my family."

Shock registered on her face for just a moment, then it was gone and a blank expression settled. "I don't know what you're talking about, Ray. Aren't we at least friends— I certainly thought so."

Ray inclined his head. "I don't know if you even know the meaning of the word."

"That's not true. How can you say such horrible things?" Tears sprang to her eyes. "A-after all th-that I've been th-through . . ."

Ray was getting tired of her antics. "Lynn, this is getting us nowhere. I'm not sure why you came here, but I think it's best you leave. In your condition, you really shouldn't be upset."

"Like you really care. This child I'm carrying—"

Ray waved her off. "Lynn, don't even say it. The baby is not mine. And don't try to tell me we had sex that one night after I got back into town. I may have been drunk, but I wasn't that drunk.''

Suddenly the tears stopped. ''If you believed all these vicious accusations, then why didn't you say something during the divorce? Maybe I wouldn't have taken everything from you. Why didn't you bring all this up then? I'll tell you why. Because you don't have an ounce of proof, that's why.''

''I have proof, Lynn, but unlike you, I didn't want to air your dirty laundry in the courtroom—against my attorney's better judgment, I might add. I didn't fight you on anything simply because I wanted to get you the hell out of my life.''

''I see. Too bad that bitch—what was her name? Oh yes, Carrie—wasn't crazy enough to sit and wait for you to come back to her.''

''She deserved better than someone like me anyway. I'll never forgive you for going through my mail and destroying her letter. I'd already agreed to marry you.''

Lynette shrugged. ''I simply did what I had to do. I was fighting for our love, Ray. I wasn't ready to just let you walk away from me. I could tell when we talked on the phone that you'd met someone. I couldn't just drop everything and hop on the midnight train to Georgia, so I did the next best thing.''

''You disgust me.''

''Our marriage could have been a good one. You never gave it a chance. And you want to know why I destroyed that letter? She didn't pledge her undying love, if that's what you think. Instead she chose to tell you how much she hated you for using her.''

''You're just looking for an excuse for what you did.''

''I may have had an affair, but I wasn't in love with him. I needed someone and I wanted to get back at you. You were the one who decided you were in love with that whore.''

"As far as Carrie is concerned, I don't want to hear you call her another bitch, whore, tramp, nothing. Yes, I was in love with her. Yes, I was going to end my relationship with you, but you lied about being pregnant. Even after all your manipulations, you still chose to have an affair. Surely you can understand why I'm having doubts as to the parentage of the baby you carry.''

"It was just a matter of time before you felt like the biggest fool who ever lived. When I have this baby, I'll make sure you nor your family ever see it.''

"Get out, Lynn.''

"I'm not ready to leave, Ray. No matter what you think, I love you—''

"Yeah, right.''

"I do. I want you back, Ray. I want us to be a family.''

He snorted and looked at her as if she'd grown three heads. "I know you've lost your mind now.''

Lynette pushed him back on the couch. "We had great sex. Nobody has been able to satisfy me the way you do. We don't have to remarry, just be together.''

In spite of his irritation, Ray laughed.

"What's so damn funny?'' she snapped.

He laughed harder.

"You bastard! How dare you laugh at me when I'm pouring my heart out to you.''

"Is that the best you can do?''

Lynette slapped him as hard as she could. "You're going to regret those very words. I plan to make you regret the very day you met me.''

"I already do, Lynn. I already do.'' He pushed her gently away from him and strode to the door. After opening the door, he waited for her to leave.

She stopped in front of him, glaring angrily before shaking her head as she walked briskly toward the elevator.

On the way to Riverside, Carrie discreetly stole a peek into the compact mirror hidden deep in the recesses of her purse.

Ray chuckled. "Don't you think you'd get a better view if you go on and just take the mirror out?"

Carrie sent him a warning glare, but said nothing.

"My family's real down to earth. You don't have anything to worry about. Just sit back and relax."

"What makes you think I'm worried about your family and what they may think of me?"

He stole a glance at her. "Is that your way of saying that you're not?"

"Ray, for goodness sake! Why don't you concentrate on the road and stop trying to analyze my actions?"

"Sorry."

Carrie turned away to stare out of the window. Inside, her stomach churned. She refused to give Ray the satisfaction of knowing she was scared. Inwardly, she wondered why she even cared whether or not they liked her. It wasn't as if she and Ray were a couple—they weren't.

He pulled in front of a two-story French-style home. The front of the house looked like a parking lot to Carrie. There were at least eight cars parked in the front and in the driveway.

"Well, here we are. This is where I grew up."

It was a picture of enchantment, with its striking Palladian window and its beautiful brick facade. "What a beautiful house. Oh Ray, this is such a wonderful place. How could you ever leave?"

"It's one of the reasons I try to stay close to home. I love it here. I'd like to build a home out here one day in Riverside."

Carrie could feel the heat of someone watching her. She turned to find a woman, who could be none other than Ray's mother, watching her intently. Forcing a bright smile, Carrie waved and shouted, "Hello."

The woman walked toward them with the aid of a quad cane. "I'm so glad you decided to come. We've been waiting a long time to meet you."

Carrie glanced up at Ray with a look of surprise on her face. "What is she talking about?" she whispered to Ray.

"I guess you've figured out that this is my mother, Amanda Ransom. I've told her all about you and Mikey."

"Where is that little man?"

Carrie gestured toward the car. "He's asleep in the car. He should be waking up pretty soon. Thank you, Mrs. Ransom, for inviting us." Carrie heard someone approaching and turned. It was the young woman that she'd seen leaving Ray's apartment.

"Ray, are you just getting here?" Looking pointedly at her, she said, "Hello, Carrie."

"Hi, you must be Kaitlin. It's very nice to meet you. I have to apologize for my initial reaction, but I was mad at your brother."

Kaitlin nodded and laughed. "Honey, I know that feeling well. Come on, I'll introduce you to the rest of the clan."

"Clan?" Carrie glanced up at Ray.

Ray laughed. "Yes, there are ten of us. I have four brothers and five sisters. They are not all here though. My oldest brother, Prescott, and his family live in Michigan. Laine lives in Washington, D. C., but he's currently in New York on business, and Nyle is off somewhere with his girlfriend."

"I'm from a family of nine, myself. I didn't know you had such a large family."

A deep baritone voice surrounded her. "Yes, it's a lot of us. Hello, I'm Garrick, Ray's older brother."

He was tall and slender like Ray. He wore his hair completely shaved off. His bald head glistened in the sun. Behind her, she heard the slam of a car door and knew Mikey was up. "It's nice to meet you." He held out his hand to Carrie.

Garrick bent down to face Mikey. "Hello, I'm Garrick, Ray's big brother. And who are you?"

"I'm Mikey. Nice to meet you. Ray's gonna be my daddy."

Surprise registered on Garrick's face, but he just smiled.

Carrie was so embarrassed that she wanted to crawl under a rock. "Mikey, please stop saying that, Sweetie." When she ventured a peek at Ray, he and Kaitlin had both turned away and from their quivering bodies, Carrie knew they were laughing.

"Why don't you all let Carrie and Mikey come into the house. Let's not overwhelm them," Ray's mother suggested.

Carrie could read the amusement in Amanda Ransom's eyes. So his mother thought this was funny as well. Gazing down at the cherub smile on Mikey's face, Carrie laughed in spite of herself.

Following Ray, Carrie entered the house. There were people everywhere. A tall woman who looked like an older version of Kaitlin greeted her. "Hello, I'm Jillian. Why don't you join us in the living room. It seems the men in this family have commandeered the den."

Sitting beside her, Kaitlin said, "I'm so glad to finally meet you. Ray used to talk about you a lot."

"He did?"

Kaitlin nodded. "He sure did. It's so amazing how things turn out. Who would've thought that the two of you would end up living next door to each other?"

"I sure didn't," Carrie admitted. "I thought I'd never see him again."

"I'm sure you didn't want to see him either, after the

way things turned out," another woman interjected. "I'm Ivy, by the way. I'm Ray's oldest sister."

"To be honest, I didn't want to see him."

"I hope that's all past you both now."

"It is, but we are just working on being friends, that's all."

"Your little boy is adorable. How old is he?"

"Mikey is four years old. He's my heart."

Jillian nodded. "I can understand that. I have a daughter and she's my heart and soul. I can't imagine life without her."

Ray peeked into the room. "You ladies ready to go? We're going to send the kids out to the cars."

Ivy stood up. "We're ready." She peeked into another room. "Elle. Allura," she called out. "You guys ready? They're loading up the car."

Two young women in their twenties came running out. "Don't leave us," the one with long shining micro braids said. "Elle was finishing up my braids."

Jillian motioned for Carrie to come over. "Allura, this is Ray's friend, Carrie. And this is Allura, Ray's sister."

Carrie could feel Allura's intense scrutiny of her, so she kept her gaze steady. "It's nice to meet you, Allura."

"You're from Georgia, right? I can tell from that cute little accent of yours."

"Yes, I am."

"Georgia. And your name is Carrie?" She glanced over at Jillian as if seeking confirmation of something.

Smiling, Allura said, "I guess you're wondering what's going on."

Carrie nodded. "I have to admit I'm very curious as to why all of you seem to know so much about me."

"Ray's never stopped talking about you. I'm glad he found you again," Allura said warmly.

The one with shoulder-length hair and a caramel complexion smiled. She was soft-spoken and seemed extremely shy. "I'm Elle, Ray's baby sister. I'm glad you could join us today."

Carrie sensed Elle was sincere. Ray's entire family had made her feel welcome. "Thank you for saying that."

Allura spoke up. "So, where's that cute little boy we've been hearing so much about?"

Carrie laughed. "I think you'll find him wherever Ray is."

"Ray's very good with children—he attracts them like magnets," Ivy stated. "Has anyone seen Daisi?"

Carrie was confused. "Daisi? Is that another sister? I thought it was only five."

Kaitlin laughed. "Daisi's married to my brother Garrick. Ivy, she's with Mama."

Ray was back. "Come on, ladies. We're ready to go."

Grabbing Carrie by the arm, Allura whispered, "Ray can be so bossy sometimes."

"What's my sister telling you?" he demanded to know.

Carrie and Allura exchanged glances. "What did I tell you?"

They both burst into laughter as they followed the rest of the women outside.

That evening, Ray eased beside Carrie on the sofa. They had just returned home and she was tired.

"Come on and admit it. You had a good time today. For a while there, I thought I was going to have to separate you and Allura."

"Yes, Ray, I did. I had a nice time. And I enjoyed being with your sister. She's quite a character."

"And then some. I don't know what Trevor's going to do with her."

Carrie searched her memory. "He's Allura's fiancé, right? I heard that they're getting married soon."

Ray nodded. "Yes, in a couple of months. The second

Saturday in November. Allura's pregnant and she doesn't want to walk down the aisle with a big belly."

"Oh." Carrie glanced down at her polished nails. "Ray, thanks so much for today. Mikey and I had a wonderful time."

"I'm glad you came. I just wanted to see you laugh again. It's been a long time." His smile grew wide. "Mikey didn't want to leave Mickey's Toontown and I think you really enjoyed yourself in New Orleans Square."

Carrie sat up. Her gentle laughter rippled through the air. "What are you talking about? You did, too. We used to always talk about going to New Orleans and the French Quarter . . ." Suddenly she shrugged, her expression becoming serious. "That was a long time ago."

"I thought we should sit down and talk . . . about what happened. We need to talk about it—it's not going to go away."

Carrie lowered her lashes to hide the sadness in her eyes. "There's no need. The damage has already been done, Ray. Talking about it now won't change anything."

"I know it won't change what happened but perhaps it will give us a foundation to start over . . . at least as friends."

"Fine. I won't promise anything, though."

Ray inspected the simple but cozy furnishings. Since the last time he'd been over, Carrie had added a few pieces of colorful artwork. He'd always known she had good taste. "You've decorated this place nicely."

She was pleased he'd noticed. "Thank you."

The room grew silent, neither one of them looking at each other.

"I guess Mikey was tired. He didn't wake up when I took him out of the car and brought him up here."

Carrie agreed. "He wore himself out with all of the rides and the parade, I think." Biting her lip, she looked away. Ray aroused feelings in her that she thought long dead.

Ray grabbed her hand, pulling it into his lap. "Carrie, how long has it been since his father died?"

She tried to ignore the tingling sensations she felt as Ray gently massaged her hand. "He died before Mikey was born." Gazing into his eyes, she asked, "How d-did you know he was dead?"

"Mikey told me."

"Oh." She sat with her slender fingers tensed in her lap.

"I'm sorry. It must have been very hard for you, alone and pregnant."

"Yes, it was hard, but I managed. After all, it wasn't the first time I'd had to go through—" She clamped her mouth shut and tried to pull her hand away, but Ray refused to let go.

Ray's eyes clung to hers, trying to analyze her comment. "What are you talking about? You've been through this before?"

"Leave it alone, Ray." She leaned back and closed her eyes. "I didn't mean anything by it."

Sitting forward, he looked at her purposefully. "Carrie, I'm confused. How long were you and Mikey's father married?"

"We w-weren't married. We were engaged, if you could call it that. Look, I don't want to talk about this."

Ray pressed further. "What did you mean by going through this before? Did this happen with someone else?"

This time Carrie snatched her hand away. "As if you didn't know."

Wearing a puzzled expression, Ray asked, "What do you mean by that?"

Anger flashed in her eyes. "Don't you dare insult my intelligence. You know damn well what I mean by that." She rose in one fluid motion. "Didn't you get my letter?"

"Yes, but—"

Carrie stood before him, one hand on her hip. "And

you're still going to deny that you know what I'm talking about? About the baby?"

"Baby? What bab—" Ray ran his hand over his face. "Wait a minute . . ."

"Forget it, Ray." She walked toward the sliding glass doors. Opening up the vertical blinds, she stared out into the dark night. "I knew this was a bad idea."

Ray jumped up and crossed the short distance. Turning her to face him, he said, "Is that what you wrote in the letter? You wrote and told me that you were pregnant? You were carrying my child? It makes sense now."

Carrie was confused. "What makes sense? Didn't you even read my letter? What did you do with it—just throw it away?"

Ray shook his head, his face full of regret. "I didn't get a chance to read it. Lynette got to it first and destroyed it, but not before she read it. Once again, she lied to me." Ray sank back down on the sofa.

"What's this all about, Ray? She lied about what?"

"She told me that you wrote me to tell me how much you felt used and how much you hated me. Lynn said that you asked me to stay out of your life."

"I never wrote any of those things, Ray."

"I never had a chance to read your letter. I picked it up from my P.O. box and stuck it into my jacket. I had to go out of town and I'd planned on reading it on the plane. I never got the chance. Lynn had found it and destroyed it. I know why she lied—she had lied about being pregnant to get me to marry her and here you were—really pregnant. Damn!" He leaned forward, covering his face with his hands.

Carrie eased down beside him. "Oh my God, Ray. I've been so angry with you all this time. I'm so sorry."

Ray settled back on the sofa, pulling her into his arms. "Don't be, Sweetheart. I'm the one who's sorry. I should have been there for you. Where is the baby?" A blank expression covered his face. "Did you have an abortion?"

She was stunned momentarily by his question. "No. No, I didn't. I had my baby alone. She was stillborn." Carrie couldn't stop the tears that flowed. "She never even got to meet me."

Ray turned her to face him against her will. "Carrie." She refused to meet his eyes. "Carrie, Honey, look at me."

He watched her purse her lips, refusing still. He could see that her eyes were wet with tears. "I should have been there with you." His hands slipped to her shoulders. With effort he kept from pulling her to his chest. "Please talk to me."

Carrie shook her head, standing still beneath his touch, yet refusing to meet his eyes. His heart ached for her. She'd aged six years since the night he made love to her . . . and left her to marry another woman. Although beautiful, she looked beaten and worn out, but he remembered how she used to be. "I don't blame you for hating me, Sweetheart."

Finally Carrie looked up at him. He watched her examine his face, feature by feature, avoiding his eyes, settling at length on the side of his face. Ray could read the discomfort in her eyes. He wanted to tell her that he was here for her now, and he would help her fight the devil himself, if it would make up for the hurt he'd caused her. But he knew she couldn't accept all that right now.

Without meeting his eyes, she said, "It doesn't matter. All the apologies in the world won't bring my daughter back. I loved her so much, Ray."

"If I'd known, I would've been there with you. I don't know if our baby would have survived, but we would've had each other." Ray swallowed. Her eyes trained on his Adam's apple. Carrie was so close, and she watched him steadfastly. She felt she would know if he lied.

"You don't know how many times I wished it had been

you carrying my child. I hated leaving you the way I did. You've got to believe me.''

"Why didn't you tell me all this back then? You made me think that you were marrying a woman you loved. I felt like . . .'' Carrie couldn't finish.

"Why didn't you try to reach me a second time?''

"Because I felt if you hadn't responded to the first letter—why should there be a second. I think that's what hurt me the most. I told you about your baby and I wanted to know if you wanted to be a part of your child's life. When you didn't respond, I had my answer.''

"I didn't know, Carrie. I truly didn't know. I would have been there somehow.''

"Even though you were married?''

"Yes, I would have sat Lynn down and tried to get a divorce. We had gotten married because of a lie.''

"If she's as bad as you say, she wouldn't have given you a divorce, Ray.''

He shrugged. "Doesn't matter. I still would have been there for you.''

Pulling her closer, Ray gazed into her hazel depths. "I loved you, Carrie. You are the one I wanted to marry.''

"Ray . . .'' She wasn't sure she could handle hearing this right now.

"I still love you, Sweetheart.'' Ray bent his head to kiss her deeply. Carrie tried to pull away, but desire won her over. His kiss, warm and inviting, settled deep in the pit of her stomach.

Carrie wanted more, she needed more, but common sense made her pull away. She was not ready to deal with the implications. "I think we should call it a night, Ray.''

He pulled away slowly. "If you want.'' Running his finger gently down her cheek, he added, "I meant what I said tonight. I still love you as much now as when I saw you for the first time. Only this time, I'm not going to let you get away from me.''

Pulling her jumbled thoughts together, Carrie stood up. "Ray, please don't say that. It's too late." She walked to the door and opened it.

"Kiss Mikey for me, will you?" Ray asked.

"I sure will. Goodnight, Ray."

He leaned down to kiss her, but Carrie turned her head away.

"Goodnight, Carrie." Ray was gone.

Alone in her bedroom, Carrie digested all that Ray had told her. He didn't know about the baby. She wanted to believe him, but she couldn't. Martin had convinced her of his innocence so many times. And that all turned out to be lies.

"I can't let my guard down. You made a fool of me once, Ray." She lay down in a fetal position, thinking about the baby she lost all those years ago. Ray would have made an excellent father. He was wonderful with Mikey.

A smile played on her face as she recalled Ray putting Mikey on various rides at Disneyland. He acted every bit the proud father. Snapping pictures of Mikey and her. It was almost as if they were a real family. A real family—the one thing Carrie wanted most in the world had been denied her.

"A baby." Carrie had been carrying his child. Ray shook his head sadly. She was pregnant when he left her. Curling his fist in anger, Ray slammed it against his end table. "Damn Lynette!" Right now, he hated her with his entire being. Ray knew he would never forgive her for her treachery.

"I'm so sorry, Carrie," he whispered to the empty room. "I never knew about the baby." A thread of guilt ran through his body as he thought of Carrie grieving the death of their daughter alone. And now she was raising

Mikey by herself. Carrie deserved much better—she deserved a husband and a father for her child.

Ray vowed to himself that he would not lose her this time. He would win her love again. And when he did—they would become man and wife. She would have her family.

CHAPTER 8

Shifting his bag of groceries to the other hand, Ray held the door open for Carrie and Mikey. He openly admired the red single-breasted pantsuit she wore. As she walked, her hair bounced with every step. Smiling down at her, he said, "We always seem to arrive home around the same time."

Carrie smiled. "Hello, Ray." She leaned against the wall as they waited for the elevator.

Ray ran a hand over Mikey's head. "What's up, little man?"

Mikey held up a drawing. "I made this for you, Ray."

Admiring Mikey's handiwork, he murmured an enthusiastic, "Thanks. I know just where I'm going to hang this."

Mikey beamed proudly.

When he looked over at Carrie, her eyes sparkled with gratitude. She spoke in a guarded voice. "How are you, Ray?"

"Can't complain. How about you? Are you okay?"

"I had a lot to think about." Looking up into Ray's

smooth handsome face, she was vaguely aware of Mikey pulling on her jacket. "Yes, Sweetie, what is it?"

"Mommy, can Ray have dinner with us?"

Carrie glanced up shyly at Ray. "Well, if he wants to. He may have other dinner plans . . ."

Shaking his head, Ray responded quickly. "Actually, I'm free. I'd like to spend more time with you and Mikey." His eyes raked over her boldly. "A lot more time."

"Great. Ray's gonna eat with us."

Carrie looked up at him, her expression unreadable. "Is eight o'clock okay with you?"

The elevator came and they stepped on. As soon as the doors closed and they were on their way to the eighth floor, Ray replied, "I'll see you at eight."

For the last six years all he'd had that were dear to him were his memories of their shared moments. Now Carrie was back in his life. Ray knew he had to make each opportunity count. Few people get second chances and he was determined to make the best of his.

He'd made a grave error in judgment all those years ago, and two people were hurt because of it. Although he felt guilty where Carrie was concerned—Lynn, on the other hand . . .

"Ray?"

He found Carrie watching him warily. "Did you say something?"

"You looked like you were in another world."

His mouth pulled into a sad smile. "Actually, I was thinking about what should have been."

Carrie's expression became guarded and she looked away. Ray wasn't worried though. He would do whatever it took to convince her of his feelings for her and Mikey.

Ray made a mental note to invite Carrie to Allura's wedding.

* * *

Two hours later, Carrie surveyed her handiwork. The small dining room table was laid with a crisp white tablecloth, and had been set with plates, bowls, and platters of steaming, but simple fare, consisting of lasagna, garden salad, a platter of garlic bread, and a tall pitcher of iced tea.

Why am I going through all this trouble for Ray? This isn't a date or anything, she kept telling herself. Just two neighbors getting together for dinner. Although Carrie kept telling herself these things, she was back in her bedroom staring at herself in the mirror. She'd chosen a cocoa-colored silk wrap sweater layered over a pair of silk pants in cinnabar. Holding her hair up in both hands, Carrie decided to pin it in an upswept style to complete her look. She remembered how much Ray used to like her hair up.

The sound of someone knocking jarred her musings. After giving Mikey the okay to answer the door, she cautioned, "Don't forget to ask who it is."

"I won't forget, Mommy." Mikey, dressed in a pair of black jeans and a denim shirt, ran to the door. "Yes, who is it please?"

"It's Ray."

Mikey opened the door. Carrie's breath caught in her throat. Ray had changed into a pair of khaki-colored dress trousers and a crisp ivory linen shirt. He was so very good-looking—her heart fluttered wildly in her breast. She was treading on dangerous waters, but at the moment, she didn't care. Right now she just wanted to enjoy this little fantasy.

Carrie could tell he approved of the way she looked, and even though she kept telling herself it didn't matter what he thought—it did matter. Finding her voice, she said, "Ray, why don't you make yourself comfortable? Dinner will be ready shortly."

He rubbed his palms together as if thinking of an approach. "Do you need help with anything?"

"No, I have everything under control." She noticed he kept watching her. "What is it?"

"You look beautiful."

"You don't look so bad yourself."

"Hey! What about me? I got all dressed up, too."

Ray looked at Carrie and they burst into laughter.

"You look handsome, Sweetie Pie."

"Why don't I take little man here and go into the living room?"

"I think that's a good idea."

When everything was ready, Carrie called everyone to the table. After a prayer of thanks, she ate quietly, leery of raising her eyes, lest she look up and find Ray watching her.

Ray tasted the lasagna. He chewed thoughtfully. "This is good, Carrie. It reminds me of Jillian's."

Her hazel eyes sparkled and laughter rang from her. "That's because I used your sister's recipe. I thought I'd make this since you talked about mine so badly the last time."

"Jillian must have mentioned how much I liked hers."

Carrie nodded. "She did. But I do have a confession to make. I made this last night and put it in the freezer for Mikey and myself."

"Well, you outdid yourself. Everything is good."

After they'd eaten, Carrie cleared the table and brought out plates laden with chocolate layer cake.

"When did you make a layer cake?" Ray asked.

"You caught me again." She laughed. "I didn't. I bought this yesterday."

She watched Ray's interaction with Mikey. They got

along so well. What would her son do when Ray stopped coming around? What would she do?

Mikey talked nonstop. ". . . Mommy can cook good, huh? She's the bestest cook in the whole world."

"Yes, she's a very good cook."

For a moment their eyes held and a quiver surged through her veins.

When they finished dessert, Carrie transported the plates back into the kitchen. Ray stood in the portal of the door.

"Do you mind if I tell Mikey a bedtime story after his bath?"

Carrie shook her head. "Go right ahead. He most likely won't let you leave here otherwise."

By the time she was done in the kitchen, Mikey had had his bath and was asleep. Ray sat alone in the living room watching TV. Carrie's intent was to take a spot on the loveseat, but Ray grabbed her hand and pulled her down beside him.

"I won't bite, I promise."

"I know, Ray."

"Carrie, I did a lot of thinking last night. I am not going to lose you again. A lie kept us apart all of those years, Sweetheart." He massaged her hand with his thumb. "After losing you and what I went through with Lynn, I thought that there would never be another woman for me. What I feel for you grows stronger every time we're together. We could have something so special, Carrie."

Confusion raced through her. Ray was saying the very things she'd longed to hear. "I-I don't know what to say."

The silence stretched between them, tight and unbearable. Ray slipped his arm around her, pulling her petite body close to his. "I know Allura sent you an invitation to her wedding, but I'm hoping you'll go with me."

"Aren't you in the wedding party?"

"I am. I still want you to attend with me. My family really

likes you, Carrie. We all want to see more of you. They want to get to know you better."

"They kind of make me nervous. Your sisters have been very nice to me and I don't usually get along with women," she admitted.

"You seem to get along with your friend from Virginia. Matter of fact, you two seemed extremely close."

"It wasn't always like that, Ray. At one time, when I walked into the room, Brandeis would take off running the other way."

"Why?"

Carrie shrugged. "That's another night."

Ray nodded. "Do you remember the first time we went out? You seemed so nervous."

Carrie gave a small laugh. "I was. You took me to Emmeline and Hessie's on the island. It was the first time I'd ever been there and it was so romantic . . . Emmeline's not there anymore." Carrie sat up. "It's in the past."

"Emmeline's may be in our past, but we can make new memories—for our future."

Carrie gave a wistful sigh. "You have no idea how much I'd like to believe that." She was caught in a trap of indecision. Bright tears shimmered in her eyes as she stared up at him, silently pleading with him to understand that she couldn't say what he wanted to hear.

"Honey," Ray urged gently, "what we have is rare. It's real and it's not going to go away." His hand smoothed an escaping tendril behind her ear.

Carrie's nails made deep indentations in her palms but she hardly noticed the pain.

"Give us a chance. I want to be a father to Mikey. Hell, I feel like he's my own flesh and blood—"

She held up her hand, unable to hear anymore. "Slow down, Ray. You're going much too fast for me."

"I'm sorry, I don't mean to overwhelm you."

"It's . . ." Carrie struggled for the right words. "I can't explain it. I just need to take this one day at a time."

Ray nodded. "I understand."

Reaching for his hand, Carrie asked, "Can we please just take this one day at a time. And no promises. I've been given lots of promises only to have them broken."

"I won't push you, Honey, but I would like to take you and Mikey to the movies this weekend. Is that possible?"

"Yes, it's possible."

"Are we on for the wedding?"

Carrie giggled. "I suppose so. I always thought the last place a man wanted to take a woman was to a wedding."

"If it wasn't my sister's wedding, I'd probably think along those lines."

Carrie's eyes widened.

"I'm only teasing."

"I bet." When Carrie yawned, Ray stood up. "You're tired, so I'm going to leave now."

She stood up. Carrie wanted to wrap her arms around him and plead with him to stay but she kept her thoughts under wraps.

At the door, Ray leaned down to kiss her. Slow and thoughtful, the corners of his lips on her mouth set her body aflame. Pleasure radiated outward and she was stunned by her own eager response to his kiss. Bestowing one final kiss on her lips, Ray left, leaving Carrie feeling like she'd been transported on a soft and wispy cloud as she headed to her bedroom.

The next morning, Carrie pulled into her assigned parking space and shut off her car. Just as she was about to get out, she spotted a gleaming black Corvette a few feet away. She knew instinctively that it was the same car that had been parked across the street from the park. A quick glance at her watch indicated that she was about twenty minutes early. Bob Steele's car was the only other car in the parking lot.

Carrie rushed into the office, heading straight to Bob's office. She knocked loudly.

"Come in."

"Good morning, Bob." Carrie casually glanced around the office. Her boss was alone.

"Morning, Carrie. You're here kind of early, aren't you?"

"I, um . . . wanted to get started on some work I left yesterday."

"You're doing a good job for us, Carrie. I'm pleased."

"Thank you, Bob." She backed away from the huge desk. "I guess I'll get started then." Carrie turned to leave. Halting at the door, she turned around asking, "Do you know who drives the black Corvette out in the parking lot?"

"Black Corvette? No, no, I don't think I know anyone who drives a Corvette. Why do you ask?"

"I just thought it strange that you're the only person here, but there were two cars parked out front when I pulled up."

"Somebody just probably parked here and either left their car here or they walked somewhere. I'm sure it's nothing."

Carrie smiled. "You're probably right." As casually as she could manage, she headed back to the door. She needed to get the license number. She wanted to scream her frustration upon finding the car gone. "What is going on?"

Could her boss be involved? Carrie shook her head. No, Bob had been too good to her. Maybe it was all just her imagination. But deep down, Carrie was sure it was more than that.

Carrie picked up the phone twice to call Ray. Twice she changed her mind. She didn't know any more about the Corvette except that it was black and was a constant in her life. She chided herself for not jotting down the license plate number when she pulled up this morning.

Bob let out a long breath as soon as Carrie closed the door. His private line began to ring.

"We can't meet at the office like this anymore. This is getting crazy," he whispered loudly.

"Did she notice the car?" the voice on the other end asked.

"Damn right she did. Man, you can't let this cause you to be careless. She's not ready to see you. You should have seen her face—she's suspicious. And you don't want to get the police involved."

"Maybe if we talk to Carrie, she'll understand that all I want is to get to know Mikey."

"It's too soon. Listen to me. Give it some time. It won't be much longer."

Carrie stayed on the sidelines with Mikey as Allura and her new husband smiled for the camera. Soon the entire Ransom family was posing for pictures, followed by the groom's family.

Everytime Ray's gaze met hers, he smiled. Carrie thought he looked so handsome in the navy-blue tuxedo. Out of the corner of her eye, she saw Mikey waving at someone. Following his line of vision, she realized he was flirting with Kaitlin, who looked stunning in the pale blue silk gown. The body-hugging dress looked as if it were made for her.

All of Ray's sisters looked beautiful in their gowns. Carrie moved over to make room for Ray as he sank down beside her.

"We're almost done."

"The ceremony was nice. It was a beautiful wedding."

Carrie put her hand to her mouth and whispered in his ear. "But Prescott looked so serious when he walked Allura down the aisle. He almost looked as if he were afraid to breathe."

Ray laughed. "You should have seen him at his own wedding. He fainted."

"Naw," Carrie muttered. "Are you serious?"

He nodded. "He fainted."

Amanda Ransom ambled over, with the use of her quad cane. "Honey, we want you and Mikey in this next picture. We're taking pictures of the entire family."

Carrie glanced over at Ray, but he only shrugged and said, "You heard my mother."

She stood up and hugged his mother. "Thank you, Mrs. Ransom. Thanks for including us."

The photographer motioned for them to join the others.

After the last picture was taken, they all headed over to the Radisson Hotel where the reception would be held.

Carrie sat with Daisi and some of the other Ransom relatives. Her expression became guarded as several of the women attending started flirting with Ray.

Daisi leaned over and whispered, "Ray only has eyes for you. If he hadn't had to sit with the wedding party, he'd be right here with you."

Carrie leaned over and whispered back, "I know. He tried to get out of it earlier."

"Ray strikes me as a very loyal man."

"We'll have to wait and see about that," she said, before taking a sip of water.

"He loves you so much, Carrie." Daisi leaned closer. "You don't know what he went through with Lynette. She was horrible."

"You know, a part of me really feels sorry for Ray, but then there's that part of me that says he deserved what he got."

"Are you still angry at him for what happened?"

Carrie nodded. "Yes, I guess I am."

"I probably shouldn't tell you this, but I feel I'm partly to blame for what happened. When Ray was in Georgia, he called Garrick and me to tell us about you. He was planning to propose to you before he left. I pleaded with him not to do it."

Carrie was about to speak but Daisi held up her hand, saying, "Please hear me out. Lynette had already told me that she was pregnant. I urged Ray to do the right thing by her. She was my friend at the time, or so I thought."

"So you encouraged him to marry Lynette and dump me?" Carrie tried to control her anger.

"Carrie, I didn't think he was in love with you. I thought it was just a physical thing or simply an infatuation. He'd only known you for a few short months. He and Lynette had been together for two years. They met at my wedding."

Carrie stared down at her plate. Blinking back her tears, she asked, "Did Lynette tell you that she read a letter I sent to Ray?"

Daisi nodded. "Yes, she said you sent them a nasty letter—"

"She lied. I sent Ray a letter telling him about the baby I carried. I was the one pregnant with his child."

Daisi looked stricken. "I never knew. Did Ray—"

Carrie shook her head. "He just found out recently."

"That little lying witch!" Daisi stabbed at her chicken with a vengeance.

"You said she used to be your friend. What happened?"

"She tried to break up Garrick and me."

"In what way?"

"She told him that I was being unfaithful to him. Her marriage was falling apart and she wanted me to convince Ray to stay with her. But I wouldn't. After I played a part in their getting married in the first place, Ray was so angry with me, he didn't speak to me for nearly two years. I vowed then to stay out of their business." She waved her fork as she talked. "When I refused, she set out to make trouble in my marriage."

Ray tapped Carrie on her shoulder. "I thought I'd come say hello. See if you were doing okay."

"I've been taking care of her for you," Daisi said.

He smiled. "I knew she'd be in good hands with you." Playing with a loose curl, Ray said to Carrie, "I'll be over here as soon as I can." Watching Mikey clown around with Kaitlin, he said, "I see Mikey's having a good time."

Carrie laughed. "I think he has a crush on your sister. He's become her shadow since Disneyland."

"Kaitlin loves it." He squeezed her shoulder gently. "I'll be back." Did his eyes hold a promise of something more, or was it wishful thinking on her part? Carrie wondered.

The waiters moved around the room, removing plates from the tables. Carrie went to freshen up in the ladies' room. When she returned, Ray was grilling Daisi about her whereabouts.

"I'm so glad you're back. This man was about to bring me up on charges," Daisi exclaimed.

"I was getting worried," Ray stated sheepishly.

When the music started, they applauded as the newly-weds graced the floor. Soon other couples joined them.

Ray gestured toward the dancing couples and asked, "Would you like to dance?"

"Sure." Carrie followed him to the dance floor. She remembered that Ray was an extremely good dancer.

Wrapping his muscled arms around her, Ray pulled her close to him. Together, they swayed to the music by Luther Vandross.

"It feels so good holding you like this again," Ray murmured in her hair. When she didn't respond, he asked, "Are you having a good time?"

Carrie peeked up at him. "I'm having the time of my life, Ray."

"I'm glad." He pressed her closer to him.

The heat of desire from being so close to Ray washed over Carrie in waves. She was still very attracted to him and she sought to keep her feelings in perspective.

They danced most of the night away.

Three hours later, Ray dropped Carrie and Mikey off at their apartment and went home. It had been a long day and they were all exhausted.

She stripped off her dress and shoes and slipped on a silk robe. Carrie padded down the hallway to check on Mikey.

She found him in the living room, dressed in pajamas and watching TV. Arms folded across her chest, Carrie stated, "It's time for bed, Sweetie."

"But I wanna watch for a little bit. Please."

Carrie yawned. "I'm tired, Honeychile. I'm going to bed, but you can watch back here in my room. I don't want you up here by yourself."

Mikey jumped off the couch and cut the TV off. Hand in hand, he and Carrie headed down the hallway to her bedroom.

While Mikey watched TV, Carrie's mind drifted to Ray. She'd had a good time with him. Sleepily, she glanced over at her son. He was asleep. Cutting off the TV, she turned to her side. Mikey would sleep with her tonight because she was too tired to carry him to his room.

She turned the radio on and lay listening to Luther Vandross. It was the same song she and Ray had danced to. Their first time in six years. Her body still tingled from the contact with his. Carrie could not deny that she craved feeling his body against hers once more. She remembered him like it was only yesterday.

The six years they had spent apart had not lessened her feelings for him. But until she was sure of his feelings for her—she had to be cautious. She would not let him hurt her a second time.

CHAPTER 9

Ray helped Mikey out of his car. "How did you like the movie, little man?"

Walking between Ray and Carrie, Mikey said, "It was good. Mommy, you liked it, too, didn't you?"

Carrie laughed. "I have to admit, I had a wonderful time. You're spoiling us. Since we went to the movies on Thanksgiving Day, we've been going every week."

"I enjoy spending time with you and Mikey." Ray held the door before following Carrie and Mikey into the apartment building. "Can you believe this is a new year all ready? Time waits for no one. You've got to grab your happiness—"

"Ray!"

As Ray and Mikey neared the elevators, they were confronted by an angry woman. "It's about damn time you decided to come home, Ray. I've been waiting for the last couple of hours."

Carrie pulled Mikey closer to her while Ray glanced from one woman to the other. Carrie could tell he was angry.

"Lynette, what are you doing here? With your due date so close, you should stay close to home."

Eyeing Carrie from head to toe, she snarled, "Who in the hell is this bitch?"

Mikey turned frightened eyes to her. "Mommy?"

Anger weaved its way through her body, but Carrie maintained her composure. "Shhhh, Honey. It's okay."

Ray bent to pick Mikey up, holding him close. In a calm but firm voice, he said, "Move out of the way, Lynn. And don't even think about making a scene. Think about your baby."

"I'm not going anywhere." She turned to Carrie. "Did he tell you he was married? And that he's about to become a father?"

Carrie said nothing. She was too stunned to speak. Ray was going to be a father? Ray never mentioned that his ex-wife was pregnant.

"Stop your lies." He turned to Carrie. "I'm divorced and I'm not going to be a father. The child she is carrying is not mine."

Although Carrie didn't look at him, or even respond, when she pulled at her hand, he released it, watching her head toward the elevators.

"How dare you tell that lie. This child is yours. You're just too damn stupid to realize it." Stepping in front of Carrie to block her exit, Lynette threatened, "If I see you with him again, I'll kick your ass from here to the valley. You got that?"

Carrie looked up at her, staring straight into dark eyes filled with hate. "I think you'd better get away from me. Ray, I'll see you upstairs."

Lynette seemed stunned by the cool reply. "Who is this whore? Someone you picked up off Sunset?" She smiled when Carrie flinched.

Ray walked over to her, putting his arm around her. "Carrie, Honey—"

"Carrie! So this is the slut you wanted to leave me for?" She laughed cruelly. "You found her. Huh, I'm surprised she's even talking to you." She surveyed Carrie from head to toe. "I thought you had good taste but . . ."

Carrie had had enough. Shoving Mikey behind her, she stated, "Look Lynette. I really don't appreciate your attitude. Even if you don't have any respect for yourself, have some for my son. But what am I thinking? You don't even have any respect for the child you're carrying. If you did, you wouldn't be making a fool of yourself in public."

"Why, you little—"

Security arrived. "Is everything okay, Mr. Ransom, Miss McNichols?"

"Leave, Lynn, or I'll have you thrown in jail," Ray warned.

"I'm leaving. Enjoy your bitch while you can. Just remember, you haven't seen the last of me, Ray."

"Goodbye, Lynn." Ray put his arms around Carrie's trembling body. "I'm so sorry, Sweetheart."

"Why didn't you tell me about the baby?"

"It's not my baby."

"How can you be so sure? Lynette seems sure about you being the father."

"Lynn and I hadn't made love in months. She claimed to have seduced me one night after I'd had a few drinks. I was lucid enough to know that nothing happened that night—not for her lack of trying. I pretended to be drunk so that she'd leave me alone. It's not my child, Carrie."

She relaxed a bit, then pulled to free herself. He held on. "I'm okay, Ray. I just don't know why you never bothered to mention she was pregnant."

"Because I didn't see a need to do so. It's not my child."

Carrie was quiet when they reached her apartment. Standing outside her door, she said, "I'll see you later, Ray."

"I want to talk to you."

"Ray, who was that lady?" Mikey asked in a quiet voice.

He bent down to Mikey's eye level. "I used to be married to her, son. Everything's okay. You don't have to be scared."

When he stood again, Carrie looked up at him, lips trembling. "Not tonight, Ray."

"Yes, tonight," he insisted. "We need to talk about what happened. I can see that it upset you."

"Whatever." Carrie opened her door and walked in. Ray followed her to the couch.

"Look at me, Carrie. Let me apologize for my ex-wife." He wrapped strong arms around her.

"You already have. Quite a few times, actually." Again she tried to free herself, but he was stronger and pulled her around to face him. He took her by both upper arms.

"Apparently not well enough. Lynette is bored. She has nothing better to do than to aggravate me. Her bark is much worse than her bite, so don't let her get to you."

He held her gaze with every ounce of concentration he could muster. He watched her eyes flicker; she tried to look away, but didn't. His gaze traveled to her lips. They were still trembling.

"The last thing I wanted to do was cause you more pain. I've hurt you enough."

"She called me a bitch and a whore in front of my son. How do you think that makes me feel?"

"I told her I'd met someone when I was at FLETC. I told her I thought it was best if we didn't see each other anymore. That's when she told me she was pregnant. I didn't know it at the time, but it was a lie."

"That's when you told me you were engaged?"

"Yes. I agreed to marry her because she threatened to keep my child from me."

Carrie nodded her understanding. "But legally, she couldn't have done that."

"I know, but she would've made my life miserable. I just didn't want to jump through hoops trying to see my baby."

"According to your sisters, she still had you jumping through hoops anyway."

"Yeah, I guess she did."

A tired sadness passed over her face. "Truth be known, I guess I'm nothing more than a whore."

"Lynn had no right to call you that."

"It bothers me, Ray, that she called me a whore. I worked so hard to turn my life around. It's one of the reasons I moved out here."

Ray wore a puzzled expression. "I don't understand."

"Everybody in Brunswick thought that I was no better than a . . . than a whore. It seems that I have it written all over me. Martin used to call me a whore, too."

In her sadness, her voice cried out to him. Ray's arms ached to respond. He closed his eyes against a rush of emotions at her hurt, her pain, her vulnerability, knowing that he had caused some of it himself.

"Then they never really knew you."

"Oh, I think they knew me well enough. After I lost you, I really wasn't a nice person. I did and said a lot of things I regret."

"That doesn't make you a whore—it makes you human. None of us are perfect, Carrie."

"I was pretty easy for some guys. Matter of fact, I was easy when it came to you."

"Easy?"

"You know what I mean."

"Honey, you were a virgin when I met you."

"Yes, but it didn't take much effort for you to get me into bed. After you left, I slept with any man who wanted me."

"Carrie, you told me you loved me. I know that you did. I also believe you must have had deep feelings for the men you slept with."

"Not always," Carrie admitted. "Some of them I didn't even like or even know their last name. At that moment I didn't care. I just needed somebody at the time. You know, the night that you dumped me, I was going to tell you that I was pregnant."

Inclining his head, Ray asked, "Why didn't you?"

"Because I was hurt and humiliated. I felt like such an idiot. After that, I guess I just couldn't stand to see anyone happy."

"You're not a bad person, Carrie. I was wrong—"

"It's over with, Ray. We can't change the past, so let's just forget it." Deep down, Carrie knew she'd never forget.

Before Ray left Carrie's apartment, she'd fallen asleep in his arms. After sending her to bed, he forced himself to come home before the temptation to seduce her became too great. He wanted to make love to her, but after her surprising revelation earlier tonight, he knew it was too soon.

The ringing of the telephone jarred him into the present. "Hello."

"Ray, are you alone, or is that tramp over there?"

He ran a hand over his face, resting on his mustache. "Lynn, I'm not in the mood for this. I'll talk to you later."

"Ray, wait. I'm sorry about earlier. It's just that I can't stand the thought of you with someone else. I love you too much."

"Lynn, please—" Ray heard a gasp over the phone. "Lynn?" When she still didn't respond, he prompted again, "Lynn?"

"Ray, you've got to come over here. I just heard a noise."

"Lynn . . ." He was tired of her manipulations.

"Ray, please. I think someone is breaking in."

There was an edge to her voice, but then again, Lynette was a good liar. She could summon tears like a fountain.

Not about to be lured over to her house under false pretenses a second time, he suggested, "Then you'd better get off the phone with me and call the police."

"Ray, I need you," Lynette begged.

"Call the police. Call me after they get there and then I'll come over."

Ray hung up the phone.

Carrie yearned for more of the soft feathery kisses Ray placed on her naked body. Moaning, her body was on fire from the sensual heat igniting from his touch. She watched him disrobe, pleading with her eyes for him to hurry.

His teasing laughter only served to make her want him that much more. Ray joined her on the bed, pressing his naked body to hers. Carrie closed her eyes, savoring the feel of his hardness. When they could wait no longer, he mounted her with the urgency of all of his stored love and passion for her.

Together they floated up into the heavens, going higher and higher until Carrie thought she would explode. Just as she was about to climax, she woke up.

Sitting up in bed, Carrie drew her knees up to her chest. "It was just a dream," she whispered. It had seemed so real. She could not deny her desire any longer.

Loneliness settled in, giving her no hope for a dreamless sleep. Ray had invaded her heart once more—although Carrie finally admitted to herself that he'd always been there. Now her body craved him.

Groggily, Ray slipped out of bed and padded into the living room to see who could possibly be ringing his doorbell at one o'clock in the morning. He opened his door to find Samuel, a friend of his, standing there with another detective. "Sam, what the hell—" He stared into his friend's face. "What is it?"

"Ray, can we come in?"

Sam's face was unreadable, but Ray was sure it was bad news. "Sure." He stepped aside to let them enter. "What's wrong?"

"Man, I hate to have to tell you this. There was a burglary at Lynette's tonight. She was shot . . ."

Ray shook his head, not believing what he was hearing. "I . . . talked to her earlier tonight. She . . . . sh-she said she thought someone was breaking in. I thought she was lying."

"I'm sorry, Ray. Lynette died shortly after arriving at the hospital.

"The baby?"

"I'm sorry. She was taken to surgery but they couldn't save her or the baby."

Ray sank down onto the sofa, holding his head in both hands. "This . . . I can't believe this." When he looked up, his eyes were filled with tears. "I thought she was lying."

Samuel nodded in understanding. "Ray, it's not your fault. Lynette . . ."

"She was telling the truth. For the first time in all of the time I've known her—she was telling the damn truth. Now she's dead."

"I'm real sorry, Ray. We found one of the suspects. He was driving her car."

Standing up slowly, Ray looked around his apartment in a daze. "Thanks, Samuel, for coming by."

"You have my deepest condolences."

Ray nodded and walked the detective to the door. Leaning with his back to the wall, he massaged his temple. Lynette was gone. Dead. She was dead. I didn't want her dead, he thought. She was a pain in the ass, but I never wanted her dead.

Suddenly feeling a strong chill, he shivered and made

his way to his bedroom. Falling back onto the bed he closed
his eyes.

In his mind, he could see Lynette's beautiful face. That
face instantly became marred by hatred. He could hear
her voice so clearly, as if she were standing in the bedroom
with him, her tone accusing.

"If you'd come when I called, I wouldn't be dead. You
hated me so much that you'd let me die . . ."

"Nooo!" Ray shouted as he shot up off the bed. "I
wouldn't have . . ." Struggling to maintain control of his
grief, he forced himself to calm down. He stared long and
hard at the shadows, as if trying to seek her there. "I never
hated you, Lynette," he whispered. "If I'd known you were
telling the truth, I would've come. You've got to believe
me."

The words that drifted in the air brought on another
chill. "Like you believed me. . . ."

Walking with determined strides to the wet bar, Ray
poured himself two shots of Jack Daniels. Although Ray
normally stuck with beer, tonight, he hoped the whiskey
would dull his senses enough to block out Lynette's accusations in death.

CHAPTER 10

Carrie was surprised to hear Kaitlin's voice on the other end of the phone. "This is a pleasant surprise. How are you?"

"Hi, Carrie. I'm fine. I'm calling to see if you've talked to Ray at all today."

"No, not today. Is something wrong?"

"Well, I've been calling his apartment all day and I'm not getting an answer. I tried his office and he's not been there either."

"Come to think of it, maybe he's out of town or working. He mentioned having to go somewhere soon—"

"I don't think so. Carrie, his ex-wife was murdered last night."

"What? You mean Lynette's—"

"She's dead."

Carrie was stunned. "Oh no. I'm so sorry to hear that. Ray must be devastated." Her heart instantly went out to him. Although he and Lynette had a terrible marriage, she knew he genuinely cared for her. "He has to be in terrible pain over this."

"Could you do me a big favor and check on him please? I'm really worried about him. I'll be flying in tomorrow. Garrick's planning on coming into L.A. today to see him."

"Sure, Kaitlin."

As soon as she hung up, Carrie knocked on Ray's door. "Ray, if you're in there, please open the door. It's Carrie. Your family's worried about you and so am I." She paused but received no response, so she tried again. "You don't have to talk to me, but please call your family. Kaitlin's coming home tomorrow and Garrick's coming to see you today." Still no response. "Well, bye . . ."

She was about to leave when the door opened. Ray's eyes were bloodshot and he reeked of whiskey. His clothes were wrinkled as if he'd slept in them.

"Ray, I just heard about Lynette. I'm so sorry."

"Where's Mikey?"

"He's in his room taking a nap."

"Go on back to your place. I don't want him to wake up and find you're not there. I'm going to take a shower and shave. I'll come over in a bit."

"If you're not there in an hour, I'll be back," Carrie promised. "And I have something for that hangover."

Ray nodded. "I'll be there."

Back in her apartment, Carrie rushed to make a pot of black coffee. She knew Ray would be grief-stricken, but she hadn't been prepared for what she just saw. He must have loved her deeply, she thought. She chided herself for feeling angst over his love for Lynette. The woman was dead, for goodness sake.

"Hey, Mommy," Mikey mumbled as he strolled sleepily into the kitchen. "Can you fix me a sandwich?"

Carrie smiled. "I sure can, Honey. Why don't you go wash your face first? When you come back, I'll have your sandwich almost ready."

Mikey stared at her intently. "Mommy, what's wrong?"

"Nothing. Oh, I've got a big surprise for you."

"What is it?"

"Ray's coming over. He should be here shortly."

"Oh, boy. He and I can wrestle and then—"

She kneeled down to his height. "Slow down, Mikey. Now I want you to listen to me. Ray's not feeling very well today. So we have to take care of him, okay? Help him to feel better."

"Okay, Mommy. I can tell him a story."

"I think he'll like that. Now run on and wash that cute little face of yours. I'll put your sandwich on the table."

"I'll be right back."

Carrie made a plate of sandwiches and sat them on the table, along with a large bag of potato chips, plates, and a pitcher of iced tea. She was about to check on Mikey when she heard the doorbell.

"I'm glad you came. I wasn't sure if you really would."

Ray walked in and eyed the food on the table. "Then who were you expecting?" He motioned toward the small dinette set.

Mikey came running out. "Ray, you're here. See," he pointed to his clothes. "I changed my shirt and shorts for you."

Ray glanced over at Carrie, his eyes filled with amusement.

Turning her head to the side, she nodded up and down, her body shaking with laughter. Mikey had on a pair of Ninja Turtle cartoon shorts and a shirt with tiny Power Rangers printed all over. When she composed herself, she kneeled to talk to her son.

"Honey, you did a wonderful job of dressing yourself, but we've got to figure out a way to help you match them."

"Carrie, do you mind if I showed Mikey the way I learned?"

"No, of course not. Go right ahead."

"Do you have any construction paper?"

"Yes, there's a huge pad of it in Mikey's room. We keep it on the top shelf of his bookcase."

"After lunch, I'm going to show you my system of matching clothes."

"Oh, boy. I can't wait."

Carrie smiled. Mikey was always excited about learning new things. And even Ray seemed excited about teaching him. She watched him and Mikey as they dove into the sandwiches. Both acted as if they hadn't seen a meal in a while. For Ray, she surmised, it could be possible, but Mikey had eaten a big breakfast this morning.

"Thank you, Ray. Mikey's so proud of the fact that now he can pick out his clothes himself. I really like that system."

"My mom taught us all that system. My dad's color blind and so she used to make labels by writing down the color and pinning them to the hangers for my father before he died. Then for her children, she'd make colored labels and write down the name of the color on them."

"So you'd learn your colors and learn to read as well while maintaining your sense of style?"

Ray laughed. "Yes, I guess it was something like that."

"I'm really glad you're in my son's life. He's missed out on so much not having a father—"

"You've done a great job with him, Carrie. Mikey hasn't missed out on anything."

"Just his father. One half of who he is. I think that's a lot."

Ray grew serious.

"What is it?"

"Lynette's baby didn't even have a chance."

"Are you sure that baby wasn't yours?"

He nodded. "I'm positive. It wasn't my baby, but I still feel its loss."

"And Lynette?"

"I feel so damn guilty." He turned to Carrie. "She called me last night and asked—no, begged—me to come over. Said she heard a burglar. I thought she was lying. I told her to call the police."

"Ray, even if you'd gone over there, you may not have made it in time."

"I still feel responsible though."

Carrie nodded in understanding. "I know how you feel, Ray. When Martin died, I felt so guilty."

"Why?"

"Because I gave him a reason for coming back to ruin lives. In the end he lost his life. If I'd left well enough alone, he would probably still be alive."

"He sounds like he was crazy. It wasn't your fault."

"Yeah, Martin was that. And what happened to Lynette is not your fault—"

The doorbell rang.

Carrie was puzzled. "Who could that be?"

"I left a message for Garrick that I'd be over here with you."

"Oh, okay." She stood up and walked over to open the door. "Hello, Garrick. Come on in."

Garrick leaned his tall frame over to place a kiss on Carrie's cheek. "How is he?" he asked in a whisper.

"I think it's going to take a while for him to come to terms with Lynette's death."

Garrick nodded his understanding.

Ray stood up. "Carrie, I'm not going to stay. I want to talk to big brother here about the funeral arrangements. I don't want to do that around Mikey."

"I understand." She had forgotten that Garrick owned a mortuary. "If you need me, just call."

Ray leaned over and pulled her to him. "I'm telling you now that I need you. But I have to first close the door on the past."

"Do what you have to do. Mikey and I will be right here." Carrie pulled his head down to kiss him. "I'm so sorry, Ray."

"Let me go tell Mikey I'm leaving."

"I hope you know how much my brother cares for you," Garrick interjected after Ray left the room.

"I care for him also. I can't stand seeing him hurting so."

"Ray tried to do the right thing by Lynn—she just . . ." he shook his head. "No point in going into it now. The poor woman is dead."

When they were gone, Carrie sank down on her bed. Ray was in so much pain. Had he loved Lynn without realizing it? Or was he grieving for the child? Carrie didn't like the way she was feeling, but there was nothing she could do about it.

Ray said that he loved her. Carrie had to believe him— trust him. He'd given her a sample of what it could be like with the three of them as a family and now she hungered for more.

Alone, Ray placed a lily on the top of the polished oak coffin of his ex-wife before turning to walk away. He had already sent his family on their way. Just as he headed down the path to his car, he spied a tall slender man with a bald head moving to stand before Lynette's grave.

Ray sat in his car and watched the man take out a hand-kerchief. He had been Lynne's lover and was the father of the child she would now be buried with.

He had glimpsed the man earlier during the week, when they were at the funeral home. He had approached Garrick, asking to see his son. Ray could see the grief in his eyes as he held his dead child. The touching farewell had been witnessed by Ray's family. There was not a dry eye in the room.

The two men in Lynette's life never acknowledged each other, instead choosing to grieve privately. There was no need for conversation between the two, Ray decided.

He drove straight home, not wanting to be around anyone. Pulling into the underground parking garage, Ray sped into his assigned parking space. Folding his hand across the steering wheel, he wept loudly.

Ray heard a soft knock. Looking up, he found Carrie standing beside the car. He rolled down his window. "Where did you come from?"

"I was right behind you when you pulled into the garage. Are you okay, Ray?"

He shrugged. "I'll be fine."

"Why don't you come upstairs with me? I'll fix you something to eat."

"Where's Mikey?"

"He's visiting his friend Willie. I'm picking him up later." Carrie opened the car door and reached for Ray's hand. "Come on, Ray. We'll have lunch, and if you feel like talking—we'll talk."

Ray climbed out of the car. Pulling Carrie close, he held onto her for dear life.

Upstairs, Carrie fixed Ray a sandwich and a bowl of soup. "Are you going to be okay?"

"I'll be fine, Sweetheart, as long as I have you and Mikey in my life." Pushing away from the table, he moved to stand in front of her. "I've missed you so much. You don't know how badly I wanted to come over here. How many times I had to restrain myself from knocking on your door."

"You could've come over anytime you wanted to—you know that. I thought I was going to have to tie Mikey down because he was so worried about you."

"Do you mind if he stays with me tonight?"

Carrie's eyes raised in surprise. "What?"

"I'd like for Mikey to stay over at my place tonight. I want to spend some time with him—just me and him."

"Well, sure . . . but why? You can stay here as long as you like."

"Because when I'm around you, I can't take my eyes off you. You are very distracting." He gave her face a soft stroking.

"It's fine. It'll give me some time to catch up on my reading, and I can pamper myself."

Ray's eyes twinkled in merriment. "Hmmmm, maybe I should stay here . . ."

Wagging her finger at him, Carrie warned, "Oh, no, you don't. You can't take it back now. I'm looking forward to this." She led him over to the sofa. "Ray, when do you have to leave town? I know you mentioned it might be sometime soon."

"I leave Monday. I'll be gone for two weeks."

"I'm going to miss you. And so will Mikey."

Kissing her gently, he murmured hoarsely, "I'm going to miss you both like crazy. Kaitlin will actually be in town, so if you need anything, call her."

"We'll be fine, Ray. I haven't seen that Corvette in a long time. Maybe it was my imagination. I feel alive for the first time in a long time."

Pulling her closer to him, Ray brushed his lips against hers. "I want to make you feel that and more. I want you to feel loved."

Carrie smiled. "I'm getting there."

The next two weeks slowly crept by. Carrie counted the hours until she would see Ray. He was due to come home today and she couldn't wait to see him.

Ray was standing outside her door when she and Mikey

arrived. In one hand, he carried two dozen red roses and in the other, a huge fire truck. Grinning sheepishly, he said, "I couldn't wait any longer to see you."

Mikey's eyes grew wide with excitement. "Is that for me?" he asked, pointing to the red fire truck."

"It sure is, little man." Ray handed the toy to Mikey.

Carrie held her mouth up to meet his as he kissed her. "I'm so glad you're home, Ray. I really missed you."

"Hey, not in front of Mikey," a voice called from behind them. Kaitlin was coming toward them.

Ray handed Carrie her flowers. "Happy Valentine's Day. I know I'm two days late, but it couldn't be helped. I had to transport a suspect to Texas. I remember how much you love roses. Hello, Kaitlin."

"What? No flowers for me?" She tried to look offended and sighed loudly. "Another lonely Valentine's Day."

Carrie laughed and handed her a single rose. "Here's one for you."

"By the way, what are you doing on this floor?" Ray asked.

"Well, I thought since you were coming home today, I'd take Mikey upstairs with me. I made a big batch of homemade chocolate chip cookies and I need someone to help me eat them. After dinner, of course. I have fried chicken, macaroni and cheese, corn on the cob . . ."

"Oooh, Mommy, I want to eat with Kaitlin. She has all the food I like and cookies, too."

Laughing, Carrie nodded. "Thanks, Kaitlin. Just let me get him washed up and changed."

"I need to talk to Ray about something, so we'll be over there when he's ready."

Carrie and Mikey went into her apartment, moving quickly. She was grateful to Kaitlin for giving her some time alone with Ray. Soon, Mikey was clean and ready to go. They headed to Ray's apartment.

As soon as Kaitlin and Mikey were on their way, Ray pulled her close to him and kissed her. When his lips touched hers, Carrie felt like her world had suddenly started spinning again.

His lips opened over hers and his tongue cut off her moan. Ray kissed her harder than he intended, deeper than he intended, more passionately than he intended.

But he wouldn't have changed a thing if he could have. Except perhaps to bring her arms around his neck and press her body close to his. For a kiss, it rocked him in a most unexpected way.

When he lifted his lips, he half expected her to try to escape, but she didn't. He felt her breath catch. She held it, then expelled it. Tentatively releasing one of her arms, he tugged at her chin, and finally brought her face to his, revealing two streams of tears sliding down her cheeks. He kissed them, tasting their saltiness.

Without warning, she jerked away.

"Carrie . . . ?"

Her breathing came hard. So did his. He reached for her, but she inched away.

"What's wrong?"

In response, she only shook her head, again refusing to look at him.

Gently he grasped her by the shoulders and guided her to the sofa, where he pushed her down and settled beside her. When she still refused either to look at him or let him embrace her, he took her hands, holding onto them when she tried to pull away.

"Tell me what's wrong, Carrie." He drew her hand to his heart. "See what that kiss did to me, Sweetheart?" She flinched at the rapid cadence. He placed his other hand on her own heart. "You felt it, too."

Carrie sat quietly, neither denying what he said, nor

agreeing. Suddenly her head jerked up. She pulled her hand away from his heart annd clasped it with the other one in her lap. Ray could tell she was shaking; when he tried to gather her to him, she scooted farther away.

"I'm not the same person you remember, Ray. Falling into bed without love or marriage is something I don't want. I never wanted it, but I used to settle. I'm not settling anymore."

"I do love you, Carrie. I wish I could get you to believe me. And no, you shouldn't . . . settle I mean."

"It's just that I've been to hell and back. I'm not traveling down that old road, not with you or anybody else. Not anymore. I have Mikey to think of."

Her back was turned to him. He couldn't see the tears in her eyes, but he heard them in her voice. He wondered if he could ever erase the terrible pain he heard.

Finally, the tears subsided. Carrie turned to Ray. "I care a lot for you, Ray. I want you to know that. It's just that I have been lied to so many times—"

"Honey, I never lied to you. I have always loved you. That's never changed."

"I want to believe you, Ray. I really do. Martin told me so many lies . . . it almost cost me my life and Mikey's."

Ray sat up straight. "What are you talking about?"

"I paid a high price for love. Martin used to beat me and I stayed with him—believing his lies."

"That bastard."

Carrie placed a comforting hand on Ray's arm. "He's dead, Ray. I had nightmares for a while and I even thought I was being followed. But I realized when Lynette died, I was still hanging on to him. I needed to put him to rest— so I did. I'm finally feel free of Martin St. Charles."

"Free enough to give me a chance to win back your love?"

"Yes." And this time, Carrie knew she was ready. Ray

stood up slowly. Staring deep into her medium brown depths, he held out his hand to her.

Carrie accepted his hand and followed him to his bedroom. In the middle of the room he stopped, and his mouth claimed hers in a series of long inebriating kisses that left her weak and trembling.

Ray's hands roamed over her back, pulling her petite form against his muscular frame. His touch was addictive and a warmth spread throughout her body. "Please don't run away from me again," he moaned in her hair.

He picked her up and carried her to the bed, placing her gently on her back. "I love you so much."

Carrie melted against him, kissing his neck and chest. His hand cupped her breast and she moaned her pleasure. Ray quickly unbuttoned her blouse.

She stilled his hand. "We don't know when Kaitlin's bringing Mikey back."

"I told her we'd call her when we were ready."

She pulled his head down to hers, and she kissed him passionately, ignoring the strange fluttering in her stomach. Carrie lay back and allowed herself to enjoy Ray's pleasurable assault on her bare breasts.

Moving from beside Ray, Carrie climbed off the bed. She undressed quickly. Ray removed his clothes. Standing mere inches apart, they stood naked, eyeing one another. His arousal evident, Ray took matters into his own hands by picking Carrie up once more and laying her in the middle of the king-size bed.

Joining her, Ray kissed every inch of her body, causing Carrie to cry out in ecstasy. It had been a while for both of them and they wanted to prolong their pleasure as long as possible. Uncontrollable desire washed over Carrie and she cried out, "Ray, I need you to love me. Love me now."

Carrie offered herself to him and he accepted, filling her completely. The center of her overflowed. To her, it was a giving and taking of undiluted love. They rushed head on in the sea of rapture until they collided in passion.

Sated, they slept for an hour. Carrie woke up and glanced at the clock. She threw back the covers, saying, "Oh no, we fell asleep. Kaitlin's probably—"

Ray pulled Carrie back into bed with him. "Calm down. Mikey's fine. I'll call right now." He made a quick call to Kaitlin.

Carrie's body still trembled from their lovemaking. Shamelessly, she felt herself getting excited once more. She looked around for her clothes because Mikey would be coming down soon. She and Ray would have to find another time to satisfy their desires.

"Kaitlin says she and Mikey are having so much fun, and since this is the weekend, she'd be glad to keep him— she's going to my mother's house and Mikey can go with her. Jillian's daughter and Prescott's kids will be over there."

"Really? She wants to keep him for the weekend?"

Ray nodded. "Is that okay with you?"

"Sure."

Pulling Carrie beneath him, he said, "I told her we'd bring up some clothes later on tonight." Murmuring in her ear, he said, "Right now, all I want to do is . . ." His voice drifted to a whisper.

After spending most of the weekend alone with Ray, Carrie was floating on air. She loved him with her whole heart and believed he loved her, too. Ray would not hurt her this time. Pulling into the preschool parking lot, Carrie went to Mikey's classroom.

She found him playing with a puzzle. "Hi, Sweetie. Ready to go home?"

Mikey grabbed his backpack. "Mommy, guess what?" His eyes were filled with excitement.

"What, Baby?"

"I saw my daddy."

Carrie stopped. "Who? Ray? Honeychile, I don't think you should call Ray—"

Mikey shook his head. "I'm not talking about that daddy—I mean my other daddy."

"What other daddy?" Carrie straightened her petite form. "Just how many men picked out for fatherhood do you have?" She opened the car door to let him in.

Stamping his foot, Mikey stated impatiently. "Mommy, you're not listening to me. I saw my real daddy. The one who went to heaven. Well, God let him come visit me. I saw him and he waved."

"Wha—" Carrie shook her head and sat down in the back seat with him. "M-Mikey, slow down."

"Mommy, what's wrong?"

Carrie fought the bitter bile that rose in her throat. "T-tell me again. Who did you see?"

"My daddy."

"You couldn't have—he's dead."

"I know. But he's an angel and I saw him today." Tears filled his eyes. "I'm telling the truth. I really did see him."

Carrie pulled him into her arms. "I know you wouldn't lie about this, Sweetness. But I think you really imagined him. You want your father so bad that you imagined him, that's all."

"No, I didn't. I really saw him. So did my friend, Willie."

"Willie saw him, too?"

"Yeah."

"Is Willie still here at school?"

"He's outside."

Carrie stepped out of the car. "Come on, Honey. I need to talk to Willie."

They went to the play area and found Willie by the swings. When the little boy confirmed what Mikey had told her, Carrie leaned on a tree for support before walking back to the car.

In a daze, she drove home. Carrie felt like her world was about to come crashing down. Why won't you stay dead and leave us alone, Martin? she thought bitterly.

She had no idea how she made it home. Carrie was glad Ray wasn't around to see her like this. She was losing her mind. She had to be. There was no other logical explanation.

"Mikey, why don't you go on and take your bath? I'll make us some dinner and then we'll watch a movie together, okay?"

"Okay, Mommy."

Carrie reached over and picked up the phone. Shaken, Carrie called Brandeis.

"What's wrong, Carrie? You sound strange."

She gave a recap of what Mikey had told her. "Do you think it's possible? Could Martin be alive?"

"No, Carrie. Martin is dead. He blew up in the car. Jackson saw it."

"But Mikey said he saw him. How could that be?"

"Has Mikey seen pictures of Martin?" Brandeis asked.

"Yes, I destroyed all of them but one. I wanted him to know what his father looked like. Now I think that maybe it was a bad idea."

"Carrie, I think it's a case of mistaken identity. Maybe Mikey saw someone who looked like Martin, that's all."

Sighing, Carrie agreed. "You're probably right. I'm over-reacting."

"So, how are things with you and Ray?"

Laughing, Carrie asked, "Now what made you bring him up?"

"Oh, I was just wondering if you two had gotten together yet. So, have you?"

"As a matter of fact, we have. Brandeis, I really think it's going to work out this time."

"I'm so happy for you, Carrie. You really deserve it."

When Mikey came into the room, Carrie motioned for him to take the phone. "Come say hello to Auntie Bran."

While Mikey talked to Brandeis, Carrie strolled into the kitchen to make dinner. Brandeis was right. There was no way Martin could have survived that explosion.

CHAPTER 11

"What's the matter, Carrie? You look troubled," Bob inquired.

She stirred uneasily in her chair. "It's my son. He really misses not having a father."

"I see. Is he acting up or angry?"

"No, it's not that. This is going to sound crazy, but yesterday," her voice drifted into a hushed whisper, "Mikey came home saying that he saw his father. I tried to—"

"What did he say?"

Carrie hesitated, measuring him for a moment. "That he saw his father."

A shadow of alarm touched Bob's face. Carrie watched him warily as he sat down. "I thought his father was deceased."

"He is. But Mikey thinks he saw him across the street from the preschool. He said his father waved at him."

"Dear God," Bob exclaimed loudly.

Gesturing with her hands, Carrie explained, "I tried to convince him that it was just his imagination."

"I'm sure you're right, Carrie. It couldn't be anything

else.'' He stood up. "Maybe you should take the day off. Spend the rest of the day with Mikey. I think he needs you right now.''

Carrie nodded. "Actually, I was thinking the same thing.'' She sat slumped over with a worried expression on her face. "Maybe I'm not spending enough time with him.'' Sighing, she reached for her purse. "Thanks for being so understanding.''

"It's no problem. I have three kids of my own. Sometimes you have to be there for them. They are our priority. Now you get out of here and spend the day with your son.''

"Thanks again.''

As soon as Carrie left the office, Bob placed a call. "Man, what in the hell do you think you're doing? Mikey told his mother about your little visit.''

"I didn't think he'd have any idea what his father looked like. Don't you understand, I had to see him. He's all I have left.''

"You shouldn't have let him see you.''

"I guess you're right. I'm sure Carrie didn't believe him.''

"You'd better hope she doesn't pursue this.''

Carrie ran into Kaitlin by the elevators.

"Hi, Carrie, I was planning to call you. If you don't mind, I thought I'd take Mikey for the weekend to give you a break.''

"Kaitlin, that's so sweet, but you really don't have to do that. Mikey's not a problem—''

"Oh, I know that. I just thought instead of me sitting up in my lonely apartment all weekend, I could have some company. Please?''

"Are you sure? Did your brother put you up to this?''

"No, actually Ray doesn't have a clue. It's my idea. I'd love to have him. We have a good time together.''

"Can I spend the night with Kaitlin, Mommy? I'll be good."

"Sure. Let me get your clothes ready." Kaitlin followed Carrie and Mikey home.

Kaitlin settled into the loveseat. While Mikey changed clothes, Carrie joined her.

"Looks like you and big brother are hitting it off. I'm glad."

"Ray's a good man, Kaitlin. And he loves Mikey. He's so good for him. Especially now."

Kaitlin was curious. "Why especially now?"

"Well, this is going to sound crazy, but Mikey thought he saw his father the other day."

"But isn't he dead?"

Carrie nodded. "I took off work early today because I thought that maybe I wasn't spending enough time with him."

"He probably saw someone who looked similar to his father. You know how everyone says we each have a twin. He's as well adjusted as any child I know."

"Thank you for saying that, Kaitlin. I've tried to do the best I can for my son."

"You're a great mother, Carrie. Don't worry so."

Two hours after Kaitlin had taken Mikey upstairs, Carrie heard Ray's door open. She jumped up and ran to the door. "Hello, Ray."

His eyes shined with happiness. "What are you doing home this early, Sweetheart?"

"I came home to spend time with Mikey, but he's spending the weekend with Kaitlin." Carrie grinned. "So, I thought that maybe you could spend the weekend with me."

"Let me shower and change and I'll be right over. And don't worry about cooking. We're going out to dinner tonight."

"What time?" she wanted to know.

Ray leaned down to whisper in her ear, "Right after I . . ." His voice became a hoarse whisper.

Carrie giggled.

After Carrie and Ray returned from dinner there was a message waiting from Jackson. He and Brandeis had had a daughter. They named her Natasha Caroline and wanted Carrie to be godmother to her namesake.

She and Ray made love most of the night. While he was sleeping, she crept out of bed and showered. Just as she was getting dressed, Ray woke up.

"What are you doing dressed?"

"I was going to make a quick run to the mall and pick up a gift for my new goddaughter. It won't take long."

Ray crawled out of bed, his nakedness pleading with Carrie to change her mind.

"Come back to bed and we'll go later on," Ray suggested.

"You don't have to get up. I'll be right back before you know it. I'll even stop and get us something to eat."

"Okay. I'll stay here if that's what you want. But hurry back."

Kissing him fully on the mouth, Carrie picked up her keys and said, "I'll be right back. I know exactly what I want to get her."

Carrie drove to the mall and quickly purchased the gift and had it wrapped. Out the corner of her eye, she spied a familiar face. Carrie turned. The man was gone.

"Oh my God, it's not possible." Carrie closed her eyes and opened them. She looked around her once more but it was if he'd disappeared into thin air.

Running as fast as she could, Carrie headed to her car. She looked frantically around the parking lot, but she couldn't find what she was searching for—a black Corvette.

She sat there for a few minutes trying to maintain her composure.

"Martin is dead. It's just your imagination," Carrie kept telling herself all the way home. But no matter how many times she kept telling herself that what she saw wasn't real, her trembling fingers and nervous stomach told a different story.

Ray was dressed and sitting in the living room watching TV when Carrie arrived home. He saw the fear in her eyes. Standing up, he crossed the room in quick strides. "What's wrong? What happened?"

"I forgot to pick up the food. I'm sorry." Carrie made her way to the sofa and fell back on it.

"Honey, what happened?"

Her eyes filled with tears. "Ray, I don't think Mikey was wrong about seeing his father. I think he's here. He's come back for us." Carrie put her hands to her face and sobbed.

"Carrie, you're not making sense, here. You told me that Martin died in a car explosion."

"I thought s-so. Everyone thought he was dead."

Ray leaned forward with his hands together. "What makes you think he's alive?"

"He's the driver of that Corvette I kept seeing. I know it."

"Did you see it today?"

Carrie shook her head. "No, I didn't. But I did get a glimpse of him. I saw him, Ray."

"You saw Martin St. Charles?"

She nodded, unable to speak.

"Are you sure about this? Did you get a good look at him?"

Carrie averted her eyes. "No. I caught a glimpse of him out of the corner of my eye. When I turned for a better look, he was gone." She picked at the buttons on her shirt.

In a small voice she asked, "Do you think I'm losing my mind?"

Ray pulled her into the safety of his arms. "No, honey, I don't think you're crazy. Something's going on and I'm going to find out what it is."

Carrie freed herself from the comfort of his embrace. "What are you going to do, Ray?"

"I'm going to find out if Martin St. Charles is dead."

"I feel so silly for putting you through this—"

"This man keeps showing up too many places, Carrie. I want to get to the bottom of this." He got up and went into her bedroom. Ray returned with a pad of paper and a pen. "Okay, now tell me everything about Martin and his death. . . ."

CHAPTER 12

After work, Carrie picked up Mikey and headed straight home. Ray would be arriving shortly with news about Martin's death. She worried that Ray would find out that somehow Martin had been able to escape the explosion.

If he's alive, what does it mean? she thought. Martin never wanted her or their son. Carrie shook her head. She couldn't think like that.

"Mommy, are you feeling well? Does your tummy hurt?" Mikey asked.

Carrie hadn't been aware that he was nearby. Smiling, she said, "No, Sweetie, I'm fine. I'm just thinking, that's all."

"Are you thinking about Ray? I love him, Mommy."

She ran her slender fingers through his curls. "It's time for you to have another haircut. We'll have to see if Ray will give you one."

"How come we cain't live at Ray's house?"

"Because he and I are not married."

"Then why don't you marry him?" Mikey persisted.

"Well, Ray hasn't asked me to marry him."

"Well—"

Ray's knocking interrupted Mikey's next question. Carrie was grateful for the temporary reprieve. She stood up when Ray entered the apartment.

"Hello, little man. You're not giving your mother a hard time, are you?"

"I been a good boy, Ray."

His dark brown eyes met her hazel ones. "Hello, Carrie." Bending down, he kissed her quickly. In a whisper, he said, "Martin is dead. He died that night in the explosion."

"I guess I should be relieved, but I'm not." Carrie walked to her bedroom and closed the door.

A few minutes later, Ray found her on the bed in a fetal position. "Honey, you're not crazy. I know you saw something, but it wasn't Martin."

Carrie sat up, her face streaked with tears. "Why am I going through this, Ray?"

Ray shook his head. "I think you just need to relax a little bit. Forget about Martin and the past. I don't think you've fully let go of him."

"I can't. He's the father of my son."

"He didn't deserve a child."

Carrie could hear the bitterness in Ray's voice. "Even so, he was Mikey's father."

He sat on the edge of her bed. "I know that. All I'm saying is that the man is dead. Say goodbye to that part of your life and let go. You keep seeing his ghost everywhere because you won't let him die in your memories."

She felt herself getting angry. "Have you let Lynette die in yours? Can you forget her and what she put you through so easily?"

"Carrie, that's not . . ." Ray shook his head. "You know what? I think we need some quality rest and relaxation away from Los Angeles. What do you think?"

Her head was pounding. "I don't know, Ray."

Standing up, Ray responded, "It's obvious you cared a

hell of a lot more for Martin than you've admitted to me. Maybe this is a bad idea—us being together right now."

Carrie couldn't believe Ray was standing here angry—no, jealous was a better word, of a dead man. "Ray, I think you'd better leave."

Ray nodded in agreement. "I think you're right—then you can mourn—"

"Goodbye, whoever you are," Carrie interjected, "because you're definitely not the Ray I know."

Ray left Carrie wondering what had just taken place in her bedroom. How could he be so upset about Martin? He'd said himself that the man was dead. Carrie no longer had feelings for Martin. She loved Ray. Had always loved him. Although she hadn't told him, couldn't he see it? Couldn't he feel it when they made love? He had to know how much she loved him.

Carrie answered her phone on the third ring. "Hello."

"Sorry to disappoint you, but it's only me. Not Ray."

"What makes you think I was hoping it was Ray?" Carrie asked.

"Because I could hear it in your voice. Why didn't you go with him to Oceanside?"

"We had a fight, Kaitlin. When he asked me, I told him I needed to think about it and he got upset."

Surprise was evident in Kaitlin's voice. "He got upset over that? That doesn't sound like Ray."

"Well, it was more than that . . ." Carrie told her about Martin.

"I have to agree with you, Carrie. Sounds like he's jealous of a dead man. But it's just a big misunderstanding. Why don't you go down and surprise him? I bet the two of you can work things out."

"What would I do with Mikey?"

"Allura and Elle are coming tonight, so Mikey can stay with us."

"Are you sure you don't want to keep it girls' night? You don't need a little boy in the way."

"Mikey needs to get to know all of us. After all, you and Ray will most likely end up married—"

"I don't know about that, Kaitlin." Carrie wanted that with all of her heart but she would not get her hopes up this time.

"It's all settled then. I'll let you go so that you can get packed and on the road. It's a couple of hours away. I'll be down in a few minutes, okay?"

Carrie laughed. "You and Ray are just alike—neither one of you can take no for an answer."

"The sooner you pack and get on the road, the sooner you'll see Ray."

Thirty-five minutes later, Carrie was on the 405 freeway, heading to Oceanside.

Ray held his tennis racket in position. He'd won the last game and was intent on winning this one too. Sending the ball flying back over the net, he laughed when he heard his opponent's curse.

"I thought you said you hadn't played in years," the man yelled out. "You play like a pro."

Ray's attention was elsewhere. A petite woman strolled by the huge swimming pool a few yards away. The long, light brown hair and tawny complexion reminded him of Carrie. Shaking his head, Ray knew it couldn't be her. She'd decided to stay home and live in the past with Martin, he thought bitterly.

"Hey, you still playing?"

Ray turned his attention back to his opponent. "I'm ready." He chanced another look at the striking woman with the curvacious body and the skimpy swimsuit.

Shielding his eyes with his hand, Ray realized that it was either Carrie or her twin.

Dropping his racket down, Ray shouted, "You win, I forfeit the game." He jogged over to the pool, but by the time he got there, Carrie or whoever she was had gone. Ray had to wonder if she'd been there in the first place.

"Now I'm acting like Carrie," he muttered to himself. "I'm seeing her everywhere." Ray returned to the tennis courts and soon found another opponent.

Every now and then he would chance a look at the pool, but to his disappointment, the woman had vanished.

Carrie thanked the bellman and gave him a generous tip for letting her into Ray's room. She laughed when she thought about Ray running across the grounds toward the pool area. She'd wondered if he had seen her.

The huge king-size bed beckoned to her. Sleepy, Carrie slipped off the swimsuit she'd bought in the hotel boutique and climbed into his bed, slipping beneath the cool, comforting covers. She was asleep before her head hit the pillow.

Exhausted and sweaty, Ray made his way to his hotel suite. Somewhat shaken about seeing visions of Carrie by the pool, Ray decided what he needed was a long nap.

When he opened the door to his room, he immediately sensed that something was different. Ray eased in quietly. The bedroom door was slightly ajar. Searching his memory, he recalled leaving it open.

With practiced skill, Ray navigated silently across the room. He peeked into the room. Someone was in his bed. Holding his breath, he moved further into the room. His heart skipped a beat. It was Carrie, her long hair fanned across the pillow.

Ray quietly removed his clothes and eased into bed. He felt himself harden upon finding her naked. Ray traced the outline of her body with soft kisses. Carrie moaned.

"Wake up, sleepyhead."

She opened her hazel eyes. "Ray . . ."

"That wasn't nice, making me think I'm losing my mind."

"I missed you so much." She offered him her mouth.

"Where's Mikey?"

"He's with your sisters."

Ray sat up. "Sisters?"

Carrie nodded. "Kaitlin, Elle, and Allura."

Shaking his head, Ray said, "Poor fella. Those three women are crazy." He looked down at Carrie, taking in her beauty. "I'm glad you came."

"I am too. There's something I need to say to you, Ray. I love you. I've always loved you. I didn't want to—not after what happened."

"I want us, Carrie. You, me, and Mikey. I love him like my own son."

"I want that, too. Martin is my past. I won't ever forget him, but I don't mourn him. Like Lynette is your past. Do you understand?"

Ray nodded. "I don't want to share you with a dead man."

"You don't have to." Carrie pulled Ray down to her, kissing him. "I need you to make love to me, Ray. Right now . . ."

Ray entered her quickly. He loved her long and hard, with a passion Carrie could never have imagined. Carrie cried out his name over and over. Pressing his body deeper into hers, she kissed him fervently until he could no longer control himself.

Calling her name, Ray felt as if he'd exploded into a thousand pieces. His body went limp as he had given her everything he had. With what little strength he had left, Ray lay beside her.

Carrie snuggled next to him and together they fell into a lovers' sleep.

CHAPTER 13

Kaitlin held Mikey's hand tightly as they headed into the mall. "Why don't we grab something to eat first?" she suggested. "What do you think?"

"I think that's a good idea."

Out of the corner of her eye, Kaitlin caught sight of a muscular man about medium height standing nearby. Although he wore dark glasses, Kaitlin suspected he was watching them intently. Pretending not to notice him, she continued to talk to Mikey. "Well, Cutie, what should we eat? It's your choice."

"Can we have hamburgers? I love hamburgers."

She laughed. "We sure can."

Walking over to A & W, Kaitlin and Mikey scanned the menu. After consulting Mikey, she ordered. "I think we're going to have two bacon cheeseburgers, two orders of fries, and two rootbeers."

Scanning the open area from a table, she glanced over her shoulder stealthily and caught sight of the handsome stranger once more. She continued her pretense.

After their meal, Kaitlin and Mikey headed to the arcade. "Why don't you play a few games?"

Mikey looked up at her with his wide hazel eyes. "What are you going to do?"

"I'm just going to step outside for a moment and then I'll be back." Kaitlin bent down and grabbed his chin. "Now, I want you to stay here, okay? I'll be right outside."

Mikey rammed his hands in his pockets and shrugged. "Okay. I'll be right here. This is my favorite game, so I'll be here for a long time."

Kaitlin walked as casually as she could manage into the mall area. She wasn't surprised to find the stranger was standing outside. She nodded at another woman who stood outside. They had run into each other several times throughout the mall. With her hands on her hips, Kaitlin approached the fair-skinned man that had been following them. For a moment she was rendered speechless. He was extremely handsome. He had the greenest eyes she'd ever seen before in her life.

With unwavering determination, she straightened her back and approached him. "Excuse me, but why are you following me?"

His mouth parted in surprise at her question. He looked her up and down as if trying to make her uncomfortable in his scrutiny. Finally he responded.

"What makes you think I'm following you? Did it ever occur to you that I might have been following the lady standing next to you? What makes you think I would prefer a slender thing like you over the healthy one?"

"I stand corrected." Kaitlin managed to stammer out in embarrassment. She turned and walked away, but she wasn't through with him by a long shot. She approached the heavyset woman they were just discussing. She motioned toward the handsome green-eyed man. Kaitlin could read the challenge in his eyes, but she didn't let that deter her. "That man over there wants to talk to you."

The woman beamed. "Oh, really? I had my eye on him, too." She walked over and immediately cornered him. Kaitlin stood back watching. She caught his eye and grinned. He lightly touched the tip of his hat. His expression stated clearly he was going to find a way to get her back. She waved a quick goodbye and went in search of Mikey. When she and Mikey came out of the arcade, the man and the woman were gone.

"I have to go to the bathroom, Kaitlin."

"Okay, Cutie. Here's one right here. You go on in and I'll wait here." While Kaitlin waited for Mikey outside of the men's room, green eyes appeared out of nowhere.

"You're a real funny lady."

Kaitlin was bursting at the edges, wanting to laugh. "Oh, you again. Where's your lady love?"

"She had to go pick up her grandchildren." He held up a piece of paper with a phone number written on it. "She gave me this."

"So you scored. Congratulations."

In spite of himself, he smiled. "Why do I get the feeling that you're really enjoying this?"

Her eyes sparkled with her laughter. Kaitlin folded her arms across her chest. "I haven't a clue."

His baritone laugh was like music to her ears. "Okay, you win. The truth is—I was really interested in you. I—"

Tilting her head in a curious study of him, Kaitlin replied, "You just never expected me to confront you, right?"

Nodding, he said, "Something like that. Can we start over?"

"Hmmmm, I don't know. After all, you're already taken . . ." She cocked her head for a second. They could hear Mikey singing. Kaitlin laughed. "That's my . . . I guess you could call him my nephew. His mother and my brother are practically married."

Making a show of checking his watch, he twisted past

her saying, "I have to run. But here, take this." He handed her a piece of paper. It's my phone number." He took off like the devil himself was after him.

She did a casual one hundred and eighty. He was nowhere to be seen. Kaitlin looked down at the note. "See you later, Matt."

"Are you enjoying yourself?" Ray asked Carrie before taking a sip of his margarita.

"I'm having a great time." She took off her sunglasses, placing them on the table. She wiggled her body to the music playing in the background. "I love Oceanside."

"We'll have to come back more often then. Ready for a walk along the beach?"

Carrie cocked her head to the side. "Is that your polite way of saying that I need to walk off some of the food I've eaten?" Carrie groaned. "I can't believe I ate that much in the first place."

"It's the first time I've seen you eat more than a tablespoon. So, I'm pleased. I just thought a walk would be the best way to end our romantic getaway."

Grabbing her glasses, Carrie rose to her feet and said, "I'm ready."

Ray pulled himself up and, taking her by the hand, led her to the long strip of beach area. The heat during this time of day was bearable, so Carrie sat down on the sand and removed her sandals while Ray removed his shoes.

Together they walked hand in hand as the ocean waves played a game of tag with their feet. Carrie felt the heat of their closeness, and the softness of his touch made her feel warm and loved.

"I'm so happy we found each other again, Ray. I never thought I would ever be this happy again." Their eyes met and Ray's held hers as effectively as his arm slipped around her waist.

"I want you to know that you and Mikey are my life. I will do whatever I have to do to protect you both."

"I know that, Ray. It's one of the reasons I love you." Carrie slipped her arms around his waist.

He pushed her hair, damp from the mist, away from her face. "I want to make love to you right here. Right now."

Carrie pulled away. "I don't think that's a good idea. Especially with all these people around. Why don't we head back to the room and . . ." Her voice became a low whisper.

Weaving his fingers through hers, Ray threw back his head and laughed.

Kaitlin lay back on her bed trying to decide if she wanted to call the handsome stranger named Matt. Carrie and Ray had picked Mikey up a couple of hours ago, so now she was alone.

She tried to call to mind the last time she'd even gone out on a date. It had been, what? Ten months ago. Stunned by that revelation, she sat up. "We've got to change that. I'm not planning on being alone for the rest of my life."

Reaching for the phone, she dialed quickly. When she heard Matt's sexy baritone voice, she hung up. Her phone rang immediately, startling her. "Hello."

"Why did you call my house and hang up?"

"Who is this?" Kaitlin knew full well who was on the other end. "How did you know it was me?"

"Caller ID. How are you?"

"I'm fine. Sorry about hanging up, but I kind of chickened out when I called."

"Why?"

Kaitlin thought about his question. She decided to tell him the truth. "I'm not used to making the first move."

"You didn't. I made it. I'm the one who had to follow you all throughout the mall."

Kaitlin laughed. "So, have you called your friend?"

She heard him laugh. "No. I can't believe you set me up like that."

"You deserved it, Matt, for following me around like that."

"I'm sorry. I'd like to make it up to you by taking you to dinner. What do you say?"

Kaitlin sent up a thank-you to the heavens. "When did you have in mind?"

"How about tonight?"

Glancing at her watch, she offered, "I can meet you in an hour. Where?"

Kaitlin wrote quickly as Matt gave her the name and phone number of a restaurant in the Marina. When she hung up, she threw on her favorite Aretha Franklin tape and jumped into the shower, singing at the top of her lungs.

Her dry spell was over. She had a date.

Carrie was surprised to find Ray's door ajar. She assumed he left it that way because he had been expecting her.

"Happy Birthday."

Carrie jumped at the sound of voices unexpectedly shouting out to her. She placed a hand on her breast, as if to quiet her beating heart. "Oh, my!" Looking from Ray to Kaitlin to Mikey, she recovered quickly from the unexpected surprise and said accusingly, "You guys nearly scared me to death!"

"We just wanted to surprise you, Mommy. I didn't even know it was your birthday."

Carrie ran her fingers across Mikey's neatly cut hair. "Did Grandma call and tell you?"

"No, Ray did."

Carrie glanced up at Ray, on her face, pure astonishment. "You remembered my birthday? After all these years, you remembered?"

His eyes twinkled in levity. "I told you there's a lot I remember about you."

"I'm beginning to see that," Carrie responded.

"We got you a cake and everything," Mikey announced. "Kaitlin made the dinner. I hope you're hungry 'cause she made a whole lot."

Tears of joy sprang in Carrie's eyes. "That's very sweet of all of you. Thanks Ray, Kaitlin." She bent down to kiss Mikey on the forehead. "And you, my precious, thank you."

"No problem. This was Ray's idea." Kaitlin walked over and gave her a hug. Winking at Ray, she said, "If you don't mind, I would like to take Mikey to the movies tonight."

Carrie turned to Kaitlin. "You are going to stay here and have dinner with us, right?"

Kaitlin nodded. "Of course. I meant after the ice cream and cake."

Carrie laughed. "You're as bad as Mikey." Turning to Ray, she asked, "Would you get Mikey washed up while I help Kaitlin in the kitchen?"

"Whatever you want, Sweetheart." Ray took Mikey by the hand and they headed to the bathroom.

Carrie followed Kaitlin into the kitchen. "So, how was your date the other night?"

Her features became animated. "I had a great time. Matt is so nice. And fine. That man is fine. We had dinner then we went for a walk afterward. It was wonderful."

"Sounds like you've met a nice guy."

Kaitlin nodded. "All guys are nice when you first meet them. It takes a few months to figure out what they're really about. I'll have to wait and see what he's like in about six months."

"I wish I'd thought like that when I was younger. I

probably would have saved myself from a lot of pain and heartache." She flattened her palms against her dress.

Kaitlin made a slight gesture with her right hand. "But it's been worth it—you have a beautiful son and you have my brother. And I think it's impossible to do any better than Ray."

Carrie laughed infectiously. "I have to agree with you. Ray and I are soulmates. There is no other man for me."

Kaitlin carried the bowl of pasta out to the table. Carrie followed with the Beef Strogonoff. "This may sound really strange to you, but I feel that way about Matt, too. I don't think there will be another man for me."

"So, when do we get the pleasure of meeting this Matt?" Ray asked as he entered the room.

"I don't know, big brother. Right now, I just want to see where it goes. We're not rushing into anything."

Minutes later, everything was ready. Kaitlin called everyone to the dinner table.

Carrie wiped her mouth with the corner of her napkin. "Kaitlin, the Beef Strogonoff is delicious. This is my favorite dish in the whole world."

"I know, Ray told me. Thank you for the compliment, by the way." Rolling her eyes at her brother, she stated, "Ray stood guard dog over me until he felt it was right. So I'm glad you like it."

Carrie looked at Ray. "Did you really do that?"

He set down his water glass before responding. "I want this night to be perfect for you."

Everyone had seconds, including Mikey. When Kaitlin brought out the birthday cake, Carrie's eyes welled with tears once more. She blew out the candles after an off-key rendition of "Happy Birthday." Carrie cut quickly, giving everyone a slice of the chocolate cake with mousse filling and a buttercream frosting.

After dessert, Kaitlin quickly cleaned the kitchen and then she and Mikey left for the movies.

"I still can't believe you did all of this for me," Carrie announced when she and Ray were alone. Seated on the leather couch, she lay on his chest. "This has been the best birthday I have ever had."

"Even better than the one we celebrated in Georgia?" Ray asked.

Carrie shook her head. "No, that one is still the best."

"I guess we'll have to see if we can top that one then." He went into his room and returned minutes later. "Carrie, I meant what I said about not losing you again. I love you and I love Mikey . . ."

Carrie gazed into his tear-bright eyes, her own filling with water. "I know you do, Ray. I know." She stroked his face lovingly. "I love you, too."

"I want to do what I should have done a long time ago. I want you to be my wife. And I want to adopt Mikey. I want to be his father and your husband in every sense of the word." He pulled a small velvet case out of his pants pocket. "Will you marry me?"

Carrie closed her eyes then opened them. It wasn't a dream. Ray had asked her to marry him. Wiping the tears that fell, she covered her face with her hands.

"Honey? Did you hear me?"

She nodded. "Yes." Carrie threw her arms around him, pulling him to her. "Yes, I'll marry you. Yes!"

Later, they lay entwined in bed. Carrie admired the diamond solitaire on her left hand. She and Ray were getting married! Mikey would have the father he wanted. She wiped a lone tear and glanced over at Ray, who lay sleeping beside her.

Kissing his smooth cheek, she whispered, "I love you so much."

He turned over, pulling her down beneath him. "Then show me how much you love me." His mouth covered hers while his hand played with her breasts.

Carrie squirmed with pleasure as her body came against

his. As his sultry lips continued to tease her, she felt white hot fire kindle in her loins. She held onto the man she would marry as he carried her high above the stars and into the heavens with each thrust. She held onto him so tightly, it was as if they had indeed become one.

As Ray's thrusts became urgent, Carrie's whole body quivered under him. She moved with him until they cried out together.

Their passions spent, Carrie and Ray showered and dressed quickly. Kaitlin would be bringing Mikey home soon.

When Kaitlin arrived at the restaurant, Matt laid down his menu. "I was beginning to wonder if you were going to show up."

Kaitlin smiled and sat down. "I'm sorry I'm late. There was more traffic coming from the airport than I anticipated."

"What is it that you buy?"

She grinned. "Wedding dresses. I'm a buyer for Andrew Bridal. We have stores all over California and the Midwest."

Matt's face showed no reaction. "I see. So, do you enjoy your job?"

Kaitlin ordered a glass of wine from the waiter. "It's okay for now. I love to travel."

He seemed to be peering at her intently.

"What's wrong? Why are you watching me like that?"

"Your mole is very sexy."

The smoldering flame Kaitlin saw in his eyes pleased her immensely.

The waiter returned with her wine and took their dinner orders.

"Thank you." Kaitlin found herself studying the man sitting in front of her. "Are you always so quiet and reserved?"

Matt grinned. "I guess so. I talk when I have something to say—other than that, it would be a waste of precious air. As far as reserved, I've never thought of myself in that way."

Kaitlin settled back in her chair. "Well, you are. I've never met a man so quiet. The last time we went to dinner, I did most of the talking."

His green eyes gazed into her brown ones. "You are a talker."

She looked away, embarrassed.

Touching her hand, Matt said, "Let me clarify my comment. I like that about you, Kaitlin. You're very down to earth and I enjoy being with you."

"You like the fact that I talk too much."

"I never said you talked too much. I said you were a talker."

Kaitlin smiled. "You never told me what you did for a living. I know you said you were a photographer, but surely you have a day job?"

Matt burst into laughter.

The waiter returned with their meals.

"What's wrong, Kaitlin? You don't think I can pay for our dinner?"

"That's not what I meant. I just thought you did something more. Being a photographer seems wasted on you."

"Thanks, I think."

Kaitlin shrugged in resignation. "This is not going as well as our first date, is it?"

Matt reached over and grabbed her hand. "I'm having a great time. I love taking pictures, but I also have a family business that I inherited. I own La Maison. We have restaurants from here to New Orleans."

"I'm very familiar with La Maison." Pointing her fork at him, Kaitlin said, "I knew there was more to you than just being a photographer. You know, I almost suggested we eat there tonight." She laughed. "That would've been something. Owning all those restaurants—you must eat out a lot. When was the last time you had a home-cooked meal?"

Matt chewed thoughtfully. "Hmmmm, it's been a while."

"Next time, I'll cook you a nice home-cooked meal."

"I'd like that very much. In fact, I'm already anticipating that date."

After dinner, he followed her home. They stood by the elevators. Kaitlin grabbed his hand and said, "I had a nice time, Matt."

"I'm glad to hear that. You're good company."

"Even if I talk too much?" Kaitlin teased.

"More so. It's a relief to find someone so down to earth."

She raised an arched brow. "Sounds like you've had some interesting people in your life."

"You don't know the half of it, but that's for another time."

The elevator arrived and Kaitlin got on. When Matt made no move to follow, she asked, "Aren't you coming up?"

"Not tonight." He leaned over and kissed her cheek. "Maybe next time."

"Definitely next time. I'm cooking dinner, remember?"

Matt grinned and nodded. "Goodnight, Kaitlin."

When the elevator doors closed, Matt returned to his car, a black Corvette.

CHAPTER 14

Carrie sat down quickly before the dizziness could overtake her. She put her hands up to her face and lay back in her chair. After a few minutes, Carrie felt the wave of nausea and the dizzy spell pass. She stood up and walked over to the filing cabinet in her office.

She stood there mentally counting back to her last period. She was three weeks late. Carrie made her way over to her desk in a daze. Was it possible? Was she pregnant with Ray's child?

"Knock. Knock."

Carrie surfaced from her thoughts. "Stacy, hi. What can I do for you?"

"Just wanted to see if you'd like to have lunch with me today."

Carrie smiled. "On one condition. You let me buy you lunch."

"You got it." Stacy lowered her voice in a whisper. "I can't wait to tell you about my date with Tyler."

"From the big grin on your face, I'm assuming all is going well."

Stacy nodded. "It's going so well that you probably won't be the only one wearing an engagement ring."

Carrie stood up to hug Stacy, but the dizziness was back. She leaned on her desk for support.

"Carrie, what's wrong? You look positively green!" Stacy observed as she helped Carrie settle back into her chair.

"I think I'm pregnant."

Stacy's blue eyes grew wide. "Really?"

Carrie nodded.

"You are happy about the baby, aren't you?"

"Oh yes. It's just that Ray and I hadn't discussed having a baby so quickly."

"I know it's not my business, but didn't you two use protection? You can tell me to mind my own business."

"We used condoms and a contraceptive foam. One night the condom broke—"

Stacy giggled.

"Don't laugh." Carrie placed a hand over her mouth to stifle her own giggles. "I thought since we also used foam, everything was okay."

"I don't think you have to worry about Ray. He loves you and Mikey so much. I'm so sure he's going to love this little baby, too. I have an idea. Why don't we stop by my doctor's office before lunch? You can find out for sure if you're even pregnant."

"Thanks, Stacy."

"Well, I'd better go and finish my report. I'll see you in an hour." She was gone.

Carrie tried to concentrate on her journal entries, but her mind drifted back to her situation. Once she confirmed her pregnancy, how would Ray feel? They hadn't even set a wedding date yet. She knew without a doubt that she wanted to be married before their child was born. But what would Ray want to do?

Sighing, she returned to her work. She would find out soon enough. She was glad this was the beginning of the weekend. It would give her a chance to talk at length with Ray about their future.

As soon as Carrie and Mikey arrived home, she gave Kaitlin a call.

"Do you have any plans for tonight?" Carrie asked.

"No, what's up?"

"I need to know if Mikey can come up for a couple of hours. I want to talk to Ray alone."

Kaitlin was quiet for a minute. "Sounds serious."

Carrie nodded. "It is."

"Sure. I'll come down right now and get him."

"Thanks, Kaitlin. After I talk to Ray, I'll tell you everything."

Kaitlin gave a knowing laugh. "If you're talking about your being pregnant, I already know."

Carrie's mouth dropped open in her surprise. "How did you know?"

"Mikey was worried about you. He told me that you've been throwing up a lot. I put two and two together."

"Do you think he's said anything to Ray?"

"No," Kaitlin assured her. "I told him not to. Besides, if Ray knew, he would've said something by now. Anyway, congratulations. I'll be there in a few minutes."

Carrie hung up and headed to the kitchen. She made a peanut butter and jelly sandwich for Mikey. Suddenly feeling nauseated, she made her way to the sofa and lay down.

When the doorbell sounded, Carrie instructed Mikey to answer the door. She heard Kaitlin's voice as she entered the apartment.

"Hi, Cutie. Where's your mom?"

"She's laying over there on the sofa. I don't think she's feeling too good."

Kaitlin was concerned. "Are you okay?"

"I'm fine. The smell of the peanut butter made me queasy, that's all." Carrie struggled to sit up.

"Would you like us to stay with you until Ray gets home?"

Carrie shook her head. "You don't have to do that."

"Are you sure?"

"I'm fine." Carrie stood up slowly and followed them to the door. "Ray should be home shortly."

When they opened the door, they found him standing there about to knock.

"Why don't you ever use the doorbell like everyone else?" Kaitlin asked.

"Because I want you to know that it's me," he replied. "Where are you all heading?"

"I'm taking Mikey upstairs for a while. Carrie's staying here."

"I need to talk to you, Ray."

Closing the door behind them, Ray followed Carrie into the living room. "What's the matter, Sweetheart?"

She sat with her hands folded across her lap. Carrie was nervous. "I have something to tell you and I'm not sure how you're going to feel about it."

Ray eased down beside her. Taking her small hand into his large one, he said, "What is it?"

"Ray, I'm pregnant. I think it happened that night the condom broke—"

"You're pregnant?" Ray was clearly surprised. He ran a hand over his face.

Carrie's stomach tightened. She couldn't read his expression. She suddenly couldn't seem to breathe. If he didn't want the baby—

"Baby, that's wonderful. We're going to have a baby!" Ray engulfed her in his arms, kissing her with a passion that she'd never experienced before.

Tears of happiness welled up in her eyes. "You're happy about the baby?"

Ray nodded. "Of course I'm happy about the baby. We created that child. Our child."

"I love you so much, Ray."

Ray pulled away gently. "This doesn't mean that I'll love Mikey any less. He may not be of my blood, but he is the son of my heart."

Carrie wrapped her arms around his neck. "You're going to be a wonderful father, Ray. Mikey and I are very lucky." She lifted her mouth to his, kissing him.

"I'm the lucky one, Honey. You allowed me back into your life a second time."

"I almost didn't. If it hadn't been for Mikey, I probably wouldn't have."

"I'd like to think that I would've won you over eventually."

Carrie grinned. "We'll never know . . ."

Ray nodded toward the door. "When is Kaitlin bringing Mikey back?"

"In about an hour and a half. Why?"

Ray gave a lustful grin. "I thought we could . . ." his voice a low whisper.

Carrie giggled as he picked her up and carried her to the bedroom.

Kaitlin lay her head on Matt's chest as they stretched out on the floor in front of the fireplace. She placed her wine glass on an oblong rug edged with thick ivory tassles that lay near them.

Matt adjusted the plump floor pillows to a comfortable position. "Why are you so quiet, Sweetheart?"

"I was wondering. Why is it, you don't want to meet my family? I've invited you to family get-togethers and you've come up with excuses each time. We've been seeing each other for weeks now."

"I don't like being around a lot of people."

Kaitlin sat up. "But these people are my family. I'm very close to my family."

"I understand that. I'll meet them eventually. There's no getting around it."

Her eyes flashed anger. "What exactly is that supposed to mean, Matt?"

Matt sat up and pulled her to face him. "Kaitlin, I thought you knew this, but obviously you don't. I intend to make you my wife."

Kaitlin's mouth dropped open. She stared into his ice green eyes. She knew what she saw there mirrored her own. Matt loved her. "I . . ."

"I love you, Kaitlin. And I know you love me, too. Marriage is in our future." He ran a finger down the side of her face. "One day, you will become my wife."

Having found her voice, Kaitlin asked, "How can you be so sure? Things happen and people change. Some even turn out to be what you least expected."

"Our hearts speak to one another. I can hear it and so can you." He reached for her. "You're mine."

Pulling his head to hers, Kaitlin covered his mouth with her own, kissing him hungrily. Heat rippled under her skin as she recognized the flush of sexual desire she hadn't felt for months. The dormant sexuality of her body had been awakened.

Raising his mouth from hers, Matt gazed into her eyes. He took her hands and placed them on his chest, encouraging her to explore.

Aroused, Kaitlin drew herself closer to him, unbuttoning his shirt. She removed his shirt and admired the beauty of his smooth muscled chest.

Reclaiming her lips, Matt crushed her to him. His tongue sent shivers of desire racing through her. His hand pulled up her top and fondled her breast. Easing the lacy cup aside, he teased a taut nipple with his fingers. Kaitlin couldn't control the outcry of delight. The stroking of his fingers sent jolts of pleasure through her.

Matt released her long enough to free her of her top and bra. He eased her down on the pillows, his hands moving magically over her breasts, and continued to travel down her abdomen and onto her thigh.

Her skirt crept up as Matt continued his passionate tour of her body.

Kaitlin reached for his belt and tried to take it off him with trembling fingers. Sensing her frustration, Matt pulled away and stood up. He removed the belt and pants with quick adeptness. He was about to reclaim his spot beside her on the floor, but Kaitlin stopped him.

"No. Take those off, too." She pointed to the black bikini briefs he wore. "I want to see all of you." Kaitlin stared hungrily at the evidence of his arousal.

Totally naked, Matt joined Kaitlin on the floor. Lifting her hips, he removed her skirt and panties. Reaching over, he ripped a tassle from the rug. With it, he teasingly traced a path over her skin until she lay panting, her chest heaving.

When he used the tassle to caress the skin of her thigh, passion pounded the blood through Kaitlin's heart, chest, and head. Matt's expert touch sent her to even higher levels of ecstasy and she cried out her release.

She watched as he prepared to protect them both. With love flowing in her like warm honey, Kaitlin welcomed him into her body.

Together they found the tempo that bound their bodies together. The pleasure they found was pure and explosive. They rode the hot tide of passion that raged through both of them until they both felt the flooding of uncontrollable ecstasy.

* * *

Matt dressed quietly. Tonight had been wonderful and he'd meant everything he had said to Kaitlin. He loved her beyond reason.

His body still tingled from their lovemaking, causing him to feel a thread of guilt. He hadn't meant for this to happen until after he'd told Kaitlin everything. About Carrie and Mikey. Everything.

He heard her stir and smiled. She looked so sexy as she lay sleeping. Matt felt himself harden but resisted getting back into bed with her. He had to find a way to tell her the truth.

Matt walked silently across the room. He stood by her door looking down. He knew Kaitlin expected him to be there in the morning. Why was he sneaking out in the middle of the night? Because he couldn't risk Carrie or Kaitlin's brother finding him here. With one last look of regret, Matt eased down the hallway and out of the apartment.

CHAPTER 15

Kaitlin debated whether or not to answer the phone. She had a feeling it was Matt. "Hello," she said in a matter-of-fact tone.

"Sweetheart, it's me."

"What do you want? I figured you had nothing more to say to me, creeping out in the dark of night like you did," she sniped.

"I know you're upset because I left in the middle of the night—"

"You're damn right I am. Do you know how you made me feel? Like I was nothing more than a booty call."

"I'm sorry I made you feel that way. I just realized I had some work to do and I needed to get home. Can I make it up to you?"

Kaitlin gave it some thought. "You can at least spend the night with me the next time we get together—that is, if there is a next time."

"What are you doing this evening? I'd like to see you."

"I'll be at the store in Century City most of the day, but

I should be home by seven-thirty." She cursed herself for being so available to him.

"I'll see you around nine o'clock then."

"I'll see you then. I've got to go. I need to stop by my brother's apartment."

"I meant what I said, Kaitlin. I meant all of it."

"I'll see you later." She hung up, grabbed her keys and headed out the door.

Carrie and Mikey were at the elevators when Kaitlin arrived on the eighth floor. "Kaitlin, hello."

"How are you feeling, Carrie?"

"Much better now that I'm past the morning sickness stage."

"Mommy's having a baby," Mikey announced.

"Yes, I know, Cutie." She turned to Carrie. "I wanted to take Mikey to Knott's Berry Farm this weekend, if you and Ray don't mind. Jillian and Daisi are taking their kids. I thought Mikey would enjoy going too."

Carrie nodded. "Jillian mentioned it the other night when she called. I told her I'd think about it but I just don't feel up to going."

"I don't mind taking him." Kaitlin glanced at her watch. "Well, I have to be going but we'll talk later."

"We're on our way out, too."

Grinning, Kaitlin asked, "Have you guys set a wedding date? Let me know what type of dress you have in mind. I found some great ones, this last buying trip."

Carrie nodded with a smile. "We're getting married in about a month."

"What are you guys waiting for? I thought you would've been married by now."

"We'd planned to, but I was so sick during the first trimester, I couldn't think about planning a wedding. I did well just making it to work everyday. Besides, we're not having a big wedding. I don't want the long traditional gown and all that fluff. Just a nice dress. We're going to have a small ceremony. Just family and close friends.''

"Okay." She was thoughtful. "Hmmmm, I think I have just the dress for you. You're not really showing but I'd better take your measurements again. I'll do it this weekend.''

"Okay. Have a good day.''

"You, too," Kaitlin yelled back as she rushed off.

Carrie and Mikey headed to their car.

"I've never seen a photographer who was camera shy," Kaitlin teased as she snapped pictures of Matt.

"I just don't like to be in pictures. Come on, Honey. No more.'' Matt placed his hands to his face.

"Okay. But if none of these turn out, then I'm going to have to take some more.''

Pulling her into his arms, Matt teased, "I guess I'm going to have to buy you a real camera.''

"Why? I like my Polaroids." She leaned over to survey her handiwork. "See, look at that, Matt," she chided. "All I got is your hands flailing everywhere. You can't really see your face.''

"If you want a picture, I'll give you one. Forget that Polaroid camera.'' He wrestled the camera out of her hand and tossed it on the nightstand with the photos. Pictures went flying everywhere.

Kaitlin stood with her hands on her hips and shook her head. "Now look what you did. Some of them were still developing.''

Matt laughed and picked them up. "It's not like they are worth looking at anyway.'' He placed them back on the nightstand. "These should all be thrown in the trash.''

"Well, if you hadn't acted so silly, they would've come out real nice. You're a very handsome man.''

"We'll do it another time, okay? With a real camera."

"I suppose so," Kaitlin sighed.

"What's with the pictures, anyway? Why is this so important?"

"Well, you won't come around to meet my family and so everyone thinks I've invented a man."

He threw back his head and laughed.

"It's not funny, Matt," Kaitlin grumbled.

"I'm sorry, Baby. I'll tell you what—next month, we'll have a big dinner at La Maison. Invite all of your family."

Kaitlin's eyes lit up with excitement. "Actually, Matt, that's a wonderful idea. Ray and Carrie are getting married next month. We can have a reception for them."

"They're getting married?"

"Yes, they've been engaged for a couple of months and she's pregnant—"

"Pregnant?"

"Yes," Kaitlin rattled on. "This is so exciting. She and Ray met about seven years ago. They broke up and thought they'd never see each other again. Then she moves out here and ends up living right next door to him." Kaitlin nodded. "They were meant to be together and this time nothing can tear them apart."

Matt said nothing, his expression blank. He lay back on the bed, one arm under his head. Kaitlin watched him for a minute. "What's wrong?" she asked.

"Nothing's wrong." He raised his other hand to stroke her breast. When Kaitlin moaned, he smiled.

She crawled off the bed and undressed. When she returned, she straddled a partially clothed Matt. He'd removed his shirt earlier. Bending over, she placed a full breast in his mouth.

Matt moved from under her and lifted his hips to remove his pants. Soon, he too was naked. Instead of climbing into bed he ran out of the room and down the darkened hallway.

Kaitlin laughed because she knew where he was going. When he returned, Matt held up an ivory-colored tassle.

"You're going to have to buy me a new rug. It's getting kind of hard to explain where my tassles are going."

Matt laughed as he covered her body with kisses.

They made love until the early morning. While Kaitlin slept, Matt eased out of bed. He gathered up the photographs and hid them in his overnight bag. He didn't want to risk the chance of Carrie finding the pictures. Even though he'd covered his face with his hands, Matt would feel better if the pictures were destroyed.

Matt frowned. He'd thought for sure that Kaitlin had been able to snap one clear shot of him, but apparently not. All of the photos showed him covering his face.

When Kaitlin turned over on her stomach, Matt returned to bed, easing beside her. She snuggled close to him and Matt shut his eyes.

On Sunday afternoon, Kaitlin opened the door to let Carrie and Ray enter. "You guys are back early. Mikey, go get your shoes, Cutie."

"I'll be right back," Mikey called out as he took off running down the hall.

"Walk, Sweetie," Carrie chided. She took a seat at the glass dining room table. "How was he?"

"Sweet as always. Mikey is the best behaved child I know. He's a joy to babysit. Now Prescott's boys . . ." Kaitlin shook her head. "No way!"

Ray laughed. "They aren't that bad. You just have to put your foot down with them."

"Mikey, did you find your shoes?" Carrie called out.

"I'm coming. I found them." He came running down the hall with his shoes in his hand.

"What have I told you about running? In a house, you walk, not run. Understand?"

Mikey nodded. He held out a Polaroid to her. "I found this picture of my daddy."

Carrie took the photo for a closer look. She gasped and dropped it. She was trembling uncontrollably.

Ray was instantly by her side. "What is it, Honey?"

Kaitlin picked up the photo. "What's wrong? Do you know him?"

"That's my daddy," Mikey announced.

"What?" Kaitlin and Ray both asked.

Looking at Carrie, Ray asked, "Is this Martin?"

Carrie couldn't speak. Fear, stark and vivid, glittered in her eyes.

Kaitlin looked from Carrie to Ray. "His name is Matthew. Matthew St. Charles."

"Is this the man you've been seeing?" Ray wanted to know.

Kaitlin nodded.

Carrie whispered. "What kind of car does he drive?"

Confused, Kaitlin stared at her. Her panic making her irritable, she demanded to know, "What does that matter? Is he Mikey's father?"

"Just answer her," Ray snapped.

"He drives a black Corvette."

Carrie gasped. "Oh my God."

Kaitlin was in tears. "Is he Mikey's father? I thought you said his father was dead."

Ray held a hysterical Carrie in his arms. Kaitlin was upset, and he searched to find a way to comfort her too. "That's what we're going to find out, Honey. I need you to do me a favor. I want you to call this Matt and get him over here. Don't let on that you suspect anything. Can you do that for me?"

Kaitlin nodded and picked up the phone. When she hung up, she said, "He's on his way."

Ray sent Mikey into the other room to watch TV.

"But why? Why is Mommy crying?"

"Mommy will be fine. Now, I need to talk to your mother and Kaitlin. Will you do this for me? I want you to stay in there until I call you out, okay?"

Mikey nodded and ran down the hallway.

Sheer fright swept through Carrie. She stood up. "Ray, Martin is dangerous. Why did you have him come over here?"

"Kaitlin, do you still have your gun?" He ignored Carrie's gasp.

She nodded. "It's locked up in the hall closet."

"I need you to get it."

Kaitlin did as she was told.

Carrie had never seen Ray like this and it scared her. Her mind was a mass of confusion right now. Martin was alive!

A chill black silence surrounded them as they sat waiting for Matt to show up. Carrie jumped and her nerves tensed immediately when she heard the intercom buzzer.

Kaitlin responded. "Yes?"

"It's me, Matt."

The hair on Carrie's neck stood up and she breathed in shallow, quick gasps. It was Martin's voice.

Kaitlin let him in and they all watched the clock. Minutes later came the familiar sound of the doorbell. She looked back at her brother before opening the door.

Ray grabbed Carrie by the arm and led her into the kitchen. They heard Kaitlin open the door.

"What's wrong, Sweetheart? You sounded funny on the phone."

Kaitlin's voice was strained and sad. Carrie knew she had fallen in love with Matt—Martin, or whoever he claimed to be. Her heart ached for Kaitlin. Carrie knew first-hand how much a betrayal like that hurt.

"I need to talk to you, Matt. I-I feel as if I don't know who you are."

''Where is this coming from—'' He stopped abruptly. ''We're not alone, are we?''

Ray stepped out of the kitchen. ''No, you're not. I'm Ray, Kaitlin's brother.''

Matt nodded slightly. ''I know who you are.''

''I guess the problem is that we don't know who you are. Would you like to enlighten us?''

''Is Carrie here?''

Kaitlin gasped. ''Oh dear God. It's true.'' She burst into tears.

Carrie walked out as if in a trance. She stopped when she reached Ray. Lifting her eyes, she stared straight into Matt's ice-green ones. For the longest time, they stared at one another.

Finally, Carrie spoke. ''He's not Martin.'' She visibly relaxed. ''I never knew Martin had a twin. But then I never knew much about the real Martin anyway.'' She made her way to the loveseat and sat down across from him. ''Why have you been following me?''

Matt sat down. ''I didn't think you could handle seeing me. Martin and I were identical.''

''How did you know about me?''

''I hired a private detective to check up on Martin. I didn't know where he was and I hadn't heard from him regarding money, so I got worried. Martin always called for money—like clockwork. I know about Brandeis, the kidnapping, everything. I know what he did to you. I wanted to make restitution, I guess I can say. Make up for what he'd done to you. Mikey is my only family.''

''Mikey is not your family!'' Ray snapped angrily.

Matt eyed Ray coolly. ''He is my brother's child. My nephew.'' He eyed Kaitlin, who sat on a bar stool in the corner. She refused to look at him. ''I want to be a part of his life.''

''You're crazy,'' Ray muttered. ''There's no way we are going to let you—''

"You have no say in this," Matt interjected. "It's up to Carrie."

"She's going to be my wife. I'm going to adopt Mikey. There's not a damn thing you can do about it."

Matt leaned back in the chair he was sitting in. "Carrie, you haven't said anything. How do you feel about this? Mikey is my only living relative. All I'm asking is to have visitation privileges. I realize that this comes as a shock to you, but my intentions are sincere. Bob Steele will vouch for me."

"You know Bob?" Her eyes widened. "It was you! You got me the job with Steele Accounting."

"I was only trying to help you. I knew Frank Matthews would be retiring and closing his office."

"I'm sorry if I'm not acting appreciative, Matt, but I feel like I've been manipulated and I don't like it. I could have gotten another job on my own."

"I understand." He suddenly seemed sad.

Carrie felt somewhat guilty. "Matt, I wish you'd just come to me—instead of following me around. It scared me. I think I recall Martin mentioning your name once . . ." Carrie searched her memory. "I think he said you were dead."

"Martin lied as a way of life—"

"Much like you," Ray interjected. "Whoever you are, I've had enough. I want you to stay away from my family. And that includes *my* son."

Matt continued to watch Carrie. "I will do as you wish, Carrie. However, I must reiterate that I'd like to visit my nephew from time to time."

He handed her a card. "I'm sorry if I've done anything to hurt you. It was not my intention."

Carrie nodded.

Ray had crossed the room and stood by the door, holding it open. "Goodbye, Matt."

Matt stood before Kaitlin but she refused to look at him.

When he tried to touch her, she pushed him away. Back straight, he made his way to the door. Turning, he glanced back at Kaitlin. "I love you, Kaitlin."

She still refused to look at him. Matt walked out the door and was gone.

Ray tried to comfort his sister, but Kaitlin pushed him away saying, "I just want to be alone." She ran to her bedroom, slamming the door.

CHAPTER 16

Mikey peeked out of the guest bedroom. "Can I come out now?"

Carrie nodded. "Come here, Sweetie. We're going to leave now." She prayed her son wouldn't notice the strained tone of her voice.

Mikey walked out of the room with his hands stuck in his pockets and a timid expression on his face. He looked from Carrie to Ray and asked, "Where's Kaitlin? Why is everybody so mad?" Touching Carrie's hand, he asked in a small voice, "Did I do something bad?"

Embracing her son, Carrie kissed his forehead. "No. Goodness no. Nobody's mad with you."

Peering up into hazel eyes that mirrored his own, Mikey asked, "Are you mad at my real daddy?"

Carrie placed her hand under his chin. "Mikey, the man in the photograph is not your father." Despite Ray shaking his head in warning, she continued, "He's your Uncle Matt. He and your father are identical twins. That's why he looks so much like him. Do you understand?"

Mikey nodded. "In my school there are two twins. Their names are Ronnie and Donnie."

Carrie gazed at Ray, her eyes full of amusement. He was angry. She could see it in his expression. Looking back at her son, she said, "Let's get ready to go to our apartment. Kaitlin's not feeling well and we don't want to disturb her."

"I'm ready."

Ray was quiet during the elevator ride to their floor. The tension between them bothered Carrie. Not able to stand his silent treatment any longer, she finally turned to him and asked, "What is your problem?"

"I'll talk to you after we put Mikey to bed." Ray ground the words out between his teeth in a tone that forbade further comment.

She bit her bottom lip as she wondered what had him so angry. Carrie had never seen Ray like this before. She hardly recognized the man she was engaged to marry.

They had been in her apartment for a couple of hours before Mikey was settled in for the night. Ray had gone in to tell Mikey a bedtime story. Emotionally and physically exhausted, Carrie headed to her bedroom.

Ray found her sitting in the middle of her bed with her knees hugged to her chest.

"Well, what is it, Ray?"

"How can you even think of letting that bastard near Mikey?" He spoke with light bitterness.

Rubbing the side of her temple with her right hand, Carrie forced herself to remain calm. "Give me one good reason why I shouldn't consider it."

"One good reason. What about the way he was stalking you?"

"Honey, he explained all of that," she responded matter-of-factly. "He's not Martin."

"No, he may not be Martin, but he and that insane man share the same blood."

His contemptuous tone sparked her anger. Carrie

jumped off the bed. "So does Mikey. What exactly are you trying to say, Ray?"

"Don't try to turn this around on me, Carrie. I'm trying to protect you—can't you see that? The man is not trust-worthy."

"What has he done, Ray? Found me a job? Will he get prison time for that?" Carrie was close to tears. "Ray, I don't know you. How can you be so nasty?" Her voice was shakier than she would have liked. "All Matt wants to do is be a part of Mikey's life—"

"That what he says. I don't believe him. I think there's more to it."

"Like what? Do you think he wants me, is that why you're so upset? Honey, he's in love with your sister—"

Ray held up his hand. "No he isn't. If he loved Kaitlin, why didn't he tell her about all of this?" He sank down on the bed, his hands to his face.

Carrie eased down beside him. "I don't know. What I do know is that those two people love each other. I just hope they can find their way back to each other."

"Like hell! If I ever see him anywhere near my family, I'll kill him."

She gasped. "Ray!"

He reached for her but she pulled away. "Ray, I have a headache and I'm not feeling well. Fighting with you is too much to deal with right now. I think you should leave."

"Carrie—"

"Please go home, Ray. I don't like this side of you I'm seeing." Tossing her light-brown hair across her shoulders in a gesture of defiance, Carrie stood with her hands on her hips. "Matt is Mikey's uncle and it's my decision—my decision only—as to whether or not he sees him."

Raw hurt glittered in his dark eyes and she felt a thread of regret for speaking so harshly to him.

He regarded her with impassive coldness. "I see." Ray

headed for the door. "Well, I guess now that Uncle Matt's in the picture, you don't need me."

"Ray . . ." Carrie called out, but Ray was gone.

Curling into a fetal position, she lay with her eyes closed, trying to keep her tears from flowing.

Ray slammed the door, headed straight for the bar, and poured himself a shot of Jack Daniels. How could he get Carrie to understand that Mikey would be better off not knowing this Matt St. Charles. He didn't trust the man.

Although he couldn't put a finger on it, Ray sensed that Matt was somehow a threat to their future. He downed the whiskey and went to pour another. Ray changed his mind and headed to his bedroom. Seeing the empty bed, Ray sighed. He and Carrie should have been making love— not fighting. She was carrying his child. She was going to be his wife. Mikey . . . Mikey was going to be his son.

Ray closed his eyes. He didn't want to lose his family. He would not allow Matt to take them away from him.

Kaitlin winced when she heard Matt's voice on the answering machine. He'd called all evening long, but she still wasn't ready to talk to him.

Each time he called, Matt would plead with her to pick up the phone. Each time, her heart yearned for him. Wiping away her tears with the back of her hand, Kaitlin knew she would never stop loving him, in spite of the way he used her.

She thought of the first time they made love and burst into heartrending tears once more. His betrayal hurt deeply. From her first look at Matt, she'd felt he was too good to be true. She should have trusted her instincts more.

Kaitlin placed a pillow over her head to smother her

thoughts. She was disappointed not only in Matt, but in herself as well. She should have been more cautious with her heart. Burying her face in the soft cushiony pillow, she vowed, "I'll find a way to get over you, Matt. I'll find a way."

Carrie gave up on trying to sleep. She crawled out of bed and padded barefoot into the living room. Craving the feel of the March night air on her skin, Carrie stepped out onto the balcony. She stood soaking in the moonlight.

"Couldn't sleep?" a voice asked in the dark.

Carrie turned. Ray was sitting in a patio chair on his balcony. Wrapping her arms around her waist, she replied, "No, I couldn't."

Ray got up and walked over to the railing. "Sweetheart, I'm sorry about today."

She smiled. "I am, too. I know this is going to take some time to get used to, Ray, but we'll work it out. And I never meant to imply that you can't make choices regarding Mikey's future."

"Tonight I looked at my bed and it looked so empty without you." He reached for her hand. "I've been thinking, why don't you and Mikey move in with me? We're getting married in a few weeks."

"Don't you think that's something we should discuss while in the same room?" She grinned impishly. "I think we should talk more on this subject in the privacy of my bedroom. Tonight."

Ray nodded. "I agree."

"I'll be waiting." Carrie stepped back into her apartment and closed the sliding glass door. She waited by the door until she heard Ray's soft knock.

As soon as Carrie opened the door, Ray wrapped his arms around her. Gathering her into his arms, he held her snugly. "I don't want to lose you again."

Carrie took his face into her hands and held it gently. "You won't lose me, Ray."

Without another word, he swept her, weightless, into his arms and carried her to the bedroom. He undressed her and then himself.

Laying down beside her, Ray's demanding lips caressed hers. The touch of his lips was a delicious sensation. He placed a trail of kisses from her mouth to her breast. Ray's tongue caressed her sensitive swollen nipples while his hand moved down to the slightly round mound of her stomach.

"Can you feel our child moving?" he asked huskily.

Carrie smiled. "Not yet. But it won't be long."

"You, Mikey, and this child are my life."

"And you are mine. Ray, I love you. Please remember that."

Carrie gasped as he lowered his body over hers. Her body melted against his, and for most of the night, her world was filled with him.

Carrie marched straight into Bob's office without knocking the next morning. Leaning over his desk, she stated, "You knew everything and you never said a thing. How could you do this to me?" Her voice trembled with her anger.

"Look—" he began.

Carrie waved away his explanation. "No, Bob. You look. Why didn't you tell me about Matt? You let me go through all that agony and you never said a word. How could you be so cruel?" She paced back and forth in his office. "And that day I asked you about the Corvette. You lied to me."

Bob rose and strode to the door, closing it. He turned around to face her. "Carrie, I didn't mean for this to happen this way. I kept telling Matt to stop following you. I told him to stay away from you until I could talk to you."

"Why didn't you just tell me about Matt in the first place? You could have told me that he was Martin's twin. I would have understood."

"I'm really sorry about the way we handled this situation. I'm very fond of you, Carrie, and I don't want to lose you."

She moved to stand by the window, looking out. "I feel like such an idiot. I'm so tired of people trying to make a fool out of me."

"I'm really sorry. We were doing what we thought was best, in light of everything that happened to you."

Carrie whirled around. "By lying to me?" She shook her head. "I don't think so." She brushed away a hot tear. "I've really enjoyed working here, Bob . . ."

He stood up then and crossed the room to stand before her. "Please don't quit, Carrie. What can I do to make you stay?"

"What does it matter if I quit?"

"You're an asset to Steele Accounting. I'd really like to keep you on." He sighed. "But if you must go, then I certainly understand."

"Right now, I'm angry. I feel betrayed by you." She gave a small laugh. "I actually thought you were my friend." Carrie headed for the door. Before she left, she added quietly, "I don't know what I'm going to do right now. I have to really think about this."

Bob nodded. "I hope you will consider staying."

"If not, I'll give you the standard two weeks notice." She left his office. For the rest of the day, she worked with her office door shut.

When Carrie arrived home, Ray was already there. Kissing him on the cheek, she said, "When I stopped by the preschool, they said you'd already picked up Mikey. Is he sick?"

"No, I just thought I'd take him out of school early and we'd spend the rest of the day together. He's having his bath right now." He checked his watch. "I thought you would've been home already."

Carrie frowned. "Why is that? I don't get home until around this time everyday."

Ray raised an eyebrow. "I thought maybe you were going in to tell Bob Steele what he could do with his job."

Carrie sat down beside him. "I spoke with him, and at the time, I was going to quit, but I changed my mind."

"You changed your mind? Carrie, what in the world is wrong with you?"

"There's not anything wrong with me, Ray. I think you're the one with the problem. This crazy jealousy of yours has got to stop."

"Tell me something, Carrie. Why is it, you can be so forgiving of Matt, but you gave me hell."

"Matt never hurt me, Ray. His brother did."

"So, I suppose you're going to let him into Mikey's life?"

"I'm going to have lunch with him tomorrow and discuss it. I'll make a decision once I talk to him."

"You have no loyalties to the St. Charles family."

"Maybe not. But my son is a member of their family."

"Is it the money? They own the La Maison restaurant chain. But I'm sure you know that."

Carrie's eyes flashed white hot anger. She took several deep breaths before saying, "I really think you'd better leave. You have lost your ever-loving mind."

"Carrie—"

He reached for her, but she retreated. "Goodbye, Ray. And don't come back until you lose that attitude."

CHAPTER 17

The next day at work, Carrie glanced up to find Matt standing in the doorway of her office. She smiled and motioned for him to enter.

"How are you?" he asked in a smooth baritone voice.

"I'm fine." She looked down at her manicured nails, pretending to inspect them. The room filled with uncomfortable silence.

Finally Matt asked, "Do I make you uncomfortable?"

Feeling ashamed, Carrie shook her head. "It's just going to take some getting used to, that's all."

"I didn't mean to scare you all those times. I just wanted to see Mikey. And make sure you were okay."

"You had me thinking I was losing my mind. I saw you in Brunswick, then—"

"You knew I was in Brunswick?"

Carrie nodded. "Yes, I saw your car one night parked across the street from my house. That's one of the reasons I moved out here."

"Carrie, I'm really sorry. Things weren't supposed to turn out like this. Bob tried to tell me—"

"Ray and I had a fight over this job," Carrie interjected. "He feels I should have quit high and dry, but I happen to love it here."

"Bob wasn't trying to hurt you. For what it's worth, he was doing me a favor. Surely Ray understands that."

"It's going to take Ray some time to get used to all this. He loves Mikey so much and I think he's afraid that he'll lose him."

"I'm not after custody, Carrie. I just want to be his uncle. He's the only family I have left."

She nodded. "I understand completely. And I'm glad you want to be a part of his life. Mikey has so many questions about Martin. Maybe you can answer them."

"Ray is upset with me because of Kaitlin, too. Carrie, I love her."

She smiled. "I know. And for what it's worth, she loves you too. She's very angry right now."

"The reason I came by was not to discuss my love life, but to take you to lunch and try to convince you to let me spend some time with Mikey."

"You're related to my son, Matt. I think it's important for him to have a sense of who he is—at least that part of him that is his father." She grabbed her purse. "Shall we go?"

Matt stood and nodded. "Thank you, Carrie. I can't begin to explain how much this means to me."

"Family is very important to me, Matt. I just hope you are not anything like your brother." She peered up at him. "My instincts tell me that you're not."

"Martin and I were always as different as night and day. The only thing we had in common was our physical features."

Carrie gave a small laugh. "I bet that alone landed you in a lot of trouble."

Matt threw back his head and laughed. "I had to run

from a lot of irate fathers during my teen years. Martin would always pretend to be me."

"Oh, goodness. You poor thing."

Matt shrugged. "I just learned to move and move fast." He was suddenly serious. "No matter what Martin was— I loved him. I want you to know that."

"He hurt you, too."

Shrugging, Matt replied, "I could take it. Enough about Martin—tell me about my handsome nephew."

Wearily, Kaitlin dropped her garment bag to the floor and punched buttons, calling an elevator to the lobby. She'd been in Phoenix, Arizona for the last week and she was grateful to be home. She was almost giddy with pleasure when the elevator doors opened. Almost there, she thought.

When Kaitlin stepped off the elevator on the tenth floor, she found Matt waiting for her. "What are you doing here? Whoever let you in is fired."

He reached for her garment bag.

Kaitlin was too tired to argue over who carried her bag. Actually, she was grateful to rid herself of the burden.

"We need to talk," Matt was saying to her. "I've got to make you understand."

"Understand what? That you used me to get next to Carrie and Mikey. Well, newsflash. I already understand that."

Matt grabbed her hand. "It wasn't like that. Kaitlin, please. Let's go into your apartment and talk."

Snatching her hand away, Kaitlin argued, "We don't have anything to talk about. Would you please just go away and leave me alone?"

"We love each other, Kaitlin. You can't deny that."

Without looking at him, she announced, "I'm moving away. I leave in a week."

"What?"

Kaitlin forced herself to look him in the eye. She wanted to see the pain in his gaze. She wanted to hurt him back. "You heard me. I have a new job and I'm leaving."

"Where are you going?" Matt asked quietly.

"None of your business."

"Please don't do this. You can't do this, Kaitlin."

She took her garment bag from him and set it inside her apartment. "I've done it. Goodbye, Matt." She moved to shut the door in his face.

Matt stuck his foot in the doorway to prevent it from closing. "I'm going to find you, Kaitlin. We were meant for each other. And when I do, you are going to be my wife."

He was gone before she could think of a response.

Ray met Carrie at the door. She lifted her mouth for his kiss. "Hello, Honey." In her hand, she carried a stack of mail.

"I just got a call from Allura. She said that she's still waiting for the instructions regarding the cake. I thought you took care of that already?"

Carrie placed a hand to her mouth. "Oh dear. Ray, I'm sorry, I forgot."

"Our wedding is a week away, Carrie."

"I know. With everything that's been going on, it slipped my mind."

He nodded. "That's right. Now that Matt's in the picture, you can't even remember our wedding. By the way, did you and Matt have a nice lunch?"

She glared at him, her hazel eyes full of reproach. "If you're going to start a fight, then I'm going to take a nice long bath and just go straight to bed." Carrie dropped the mail on the dining room table. "I don't want to fight over this any longer."

"Then keep Matt St. Charles out of our lives and away from our son," Ray said, spacing the words evenly.

"I can't do that," she said quietly.

He dropped down into a nearby chair. "Then, I think we have some things to think about before we get married."

"Are you calling the wedding off?" Carrie asked, her voice rising an octave. "Is this an ultimatum?"

"I'm doing what I think is best for our little boy and you're letting yourself be ruled by misplaced loyalty to an insane family." His expression grew hard and resentful.

"What has Matt done to you, Ray?"

"He hurt Kaitlin. And you seem to forget he nearly scared the hell out of you."

"Tell me something, Ray. Are you angry with him for hurting your little sister, or are you afraid that Mikey will love him more than you? Matt is my son's uncle. You are the only father he's ever known. For goodness sake, can't you understand that Matt is not a threat to you?"

Ray stood up. "Carrie, you can't have it both ways. Either Matt is out of our lives, or I'm out of your life."

Carrie's eyes widened in shock. "Didn't you hear a thing of what I've said? How can you—" She glanced around the room as if seeing it for the first time.

"This is not the way I want to be, Sweetheart."

Her tears fell. "Th-then w-why are you doing th-this?"

"I'm going to adopt Mikey. He will be a Ransom—not a St. Charles. Hell, he's never been a St. Charles."

"That's where you're wrong, Ray," Carrie responded angrily. "Mikey may not have had the St. Charles name, but he is of their blood. No matter what his last name will be, you can't change that. This baby I carry now will have your bloodline. Nobody can ever change that."

"Carrie, please," he pleaded with her. "Don't confuse Mikey. I want him to grow up a well-adjusted child—"

"Getting to know his uncle won't hurt him. Do you think I'd do something to hurt my son?"

Ray shook his head. "I never said that."

"Maybe not—but you certainly implied it." She wiped her tears away. "I can't do this. Do whatever you want about the wedding." Carrie ran to her room before her sobs overtook her.

That night when Ray didn't come to bed, Carrie's stubborn pride wouldn't let her seek him out. Playing with the ring on her finger, she assured herself that Ray would come to see things her way. Surely, he wouldn't let this come between them.

In the early morning light, Carrie was awoken by a noise. She shot straight up. "Ray, what are you doing?"

"I didn't mean to wake you." He was dressed already and in his hand, he carried an overnight bag.

Her heart squeezed in anguish as she realized what he was about to do. Not wanting to believe her eyes, she asked, "What are you doing with the bag? Are you going somewhere?"

"I'm going to stay at Kaitlin's a couple of days. She's leaving day after tomorrow."

Carrie lowered her head to hide her tears. "W-Why?"

"Why what?"

She raised her eyes to meet his gaze straight on. Tears slowly found their way down her cheeks. "Why are you moving out? Doesn't Mikey's happiness matter to you at all?"

"You know it does."

"How can you leave us? We're supposed to get married in a week."

"I just need some time to myself, that's all. I'll be right upstairs, Carrie."

"Is this what you're going to do each time we have a disagreement, Ray?" she asked bitterly. "Are you going to run away?"

"I'm not running away."

"What do you call it?"

"Leaving before I say something I can never take back. If you need me, I'll be at Kaitlin's." He stormed out, leaving her with a look of pure anguish.

Carrie glanced over at the clock. It was three hours earlier in Virginia. She called Brandeis.

The next day, Carrie offered Brandeis a cup of hot tea as they sat watching Mikey and Brian play video games. "I told you that you didn't have to fly all the way out here. I'm fine."

Shaking her head, Brandeis responded knowingly, "No, you're not. Carrie, I can see the hurt in your eyes. But everything will work out for you and Ray. You two love each other so much."

Massaging her temple, Carrie said, "I'm not so sure. I just don't know who he is anymore. He's so unreasonable where Matt is concerned."

Brandeis lovingly brushed a curl away from Natasha's face. "This Matt—he looks identical to Martin?"

Carrie nodded. "Yes. Except when you look in his eyes. He has kind eyes and a gentle spirit. He's nothing like Martin. Matt's very humble."

"I guess I'll have to meet him, then."

"Are you sure you want to do that?"

Brandeis nodded. "Martin can't hurt me anymore." She leaned back on the sofa to a more comfortable position with her daughter in her arms. "If Matt wants to see me, then I'm fine with it."

Carrie reached for the phone and called Matt. When she hung up, she said, "He'll be here within the hour."

"Good. For what it's worth, I think you made the right decision. It will be good for Mikey to get to know his uncle."

"Brandeis, I'm so glad you are on my side. I think Ray is going to call off our wedding because I gave Matt permission to spend time with Mikey. He actually gave me an ultimatum.''

Brandeis raised a perfectly arched brow. ''I can't believe he'd do something so drastic.'' Playing with her bangs, she added, ''Carrie, I think Ray's just kind of insecure right now. I don't think a man could love his own biological child any more than Ray loves Mikey. I don't think he wants to share Mikey with Matt.''

''But Matt's not a threat to their relationship. I can't get him to see that.''

''He'll have to come to terms with it himself. And I believe that he will.''

Carrie sighed. ''I hope you're right.''

She and Brandeis had given the boys their lunch and Natasha was sleeping by the time Matt arrived.

Carrie could tell from Brandeis's expression that she hadn't been fully prepared for how much Matt resembled Martin.

''Hello, Mrs. Gray. I know I must bring back some horrible memories for you—''

''No.'' Brandeis cut him off. ''It's nice to meet you, Matt. Please don't feel bad about the way you look—there's nothing you can do about that.''

''I feel that I must apologize for what my brother did to you. Martin wasn't used to taking no for an answer. If it was something he wanted, he merely took it.''

Brandeis nodded. ''In the end, he paid with his life. Have you always cleaned up after your brother?''

Matt seemed surprised by her question. ''I guess I never thought of it that way. When we were growing up, Martin was my mother's favorite. He was sickly. My father called him a weakling and a faggot. He would beat him constantly. Said he was going to make a man out of him. I tried to protect him. My mother finally got tired of it and shot him. She killed my father right in front of us.''

''Dear God,'' was all Carrie could say.

Brandeis placed a hand to her mouth.

"Neither one of my parents had brothers or sisters, so Bob Steele took us in. He and my father were best friends. Martin ran away a week later. I wouldn't hear from him until he needed money."

"How old were you when . . . it happened?" Brandeis asked.

"We were fifteen."

"Matt, it must have been awful for you. And Martin." Carrie shook her head. "I guess that explains a lot of things."

"I'm not telling you this to make excuses for my brother. He had a choice and he chose to be the kind of person he was. I'm just sorry you all were hurt as a result of that choice."

Carrie called her son out and introduced him to Matt. She and Brandeis watched from a discreet distance as the two bonded. She smiled over seeing Mikey's animated expressions and his giggles as he listened to Matt.

Brandeis nudged her gently. "You made the right choice, Carrie," she whispered.

"I pray it doesn't cost me the man I love," Carrie whispered back.

Carrie called Kaitlin's apartment a fourth time. Still no answer. Matt had been gone for two hours, and Brandeis and the children were en route to the hotel where she was staying so Carrie could be alone with Ray. She wanted to make things right with him.

"Where are you? You should've been home hours ago." She paced back and forth across the carpeted floor. "Please hurry home, Ray. I need to talk to you." Her headache was worsening. Carrie supposed it was because of all the stress she'd been under the last couple of weeks.

The phone rang, scaring her. Carrie ran and quickly picked it up. "Ray?"

"Carrie, it's Kaitlin."

"Oh, hi. I've been calling your apartment for the last hour. Have you talked to Ray?"

"Carrie . . ." Kaitlin's voice broke. "Ray's in the hospital. He's been shot."

Carrie stared at the phone. Putting it back to her ear, she asked Kaitlin to repeat what she'd said.

"Ray's been shot."

Fear crept through her body causing her to lash out in anger. "That's a horrible joke—"

"It's not a damn joke. Ray has been shot, Carrie."

She couldn't control the trembling of her hands. "Sh-shot? Oh dear God! NO!"

"You need to get here as quickly as you can. He's at Kaiser Hospital. The one in Bellflower."

She couldn't respond.

"Carrie, did you hear me?" Kaitlin was near hysteria. "You need to come now!"

"I-I'm on my way. I'll be r-right there." She hung up and searched for her keys. Frustrated, she fell to the floor in a heap. "Please don't let him die. Oh God, please don't take him from me," she pleaded on her knees.

Carrie hastily wiped the tears from her face. "I've got to be strong for Ray. I can't break down like this," she chanted as she composed herself. Thinking clearly, she found her keys and headed toward the door.

She opened the door and was about to walk out when the room started spinning. "Ooooooow," she cried out in pain as dizziness threatened to take over. Holding her head, Carrie doubled over and collapsed on the floor. Her headache was becoming worse. Her stomach rolled and she felt the bitter contents rise to her throat. "Not now. Somebody please help me . . ." she moaned over and over.

"I've got to get to Ray. Hang in there, little baby," she whispered. "We've got to get to your father."

Carrie tried to drag herself across the floor, but the painful contractions kept coming. Weak and dizzy, she curled into a fetal position and prayed.

In her fragile state, she barely heard the knock at the door. "Help," she called out weakly.

"Carrie?" Matt glanced down and found her on the floor. He reacted quickly. Cradling her in his arms, he asked "Carrie, what happened?"

Matt's face was blurred, but she knew it was him. "I'm sick . . ." Tears streamed down her face. "I can't lose . . . Ray. He's—"

"You won't, Carrie. Where's Ray? Is he home?"

". . . H-hospital."

"Hospital?" He wore an expression of confusion on his face. He assumed she was asking to be taken to the hospital. "I'm going to take you to the hospital, don't worry. We can call Ray from there. Now I'm going to lift you. I don't mean to hurt you—"

"Kaiser. Ray . . . at Kaiser in Bellflower. I hurt." Beads of perspiration covered her forehead. "Need to be with Ray."

"I'll call Ray as soon as we get to the hospital. I promise." He lifted her as gently as he could and carried her to the elevator and out to his car.

Weaving in and out of consciousness, Carrie had double vision, and twin images of Matt loomed before her. Confused for a moment, she called out, "Martin?"

"No, Carrie, it's me. It's Matt."

He laid her in the back seat of his car and drove quickly but safely. He'd called ahead on his car phone and knew someone would be waiting for them when they arrived.

Carrie lay quietly. Every once in a while, she would cry out as her contractions came closer together. She was only six months. The baby couldn't come this early. Carrie was scared and she needed Ray. Ray. Ray had been shot. He needed her.

She struggled to try to sit up, but pain stabbed through her body everytime she moved. She felt the car turn into a driveway and assumed they had arrived at the hospital.

The door opened quickly and two women assisted Matt in placing her on a gurney. She was wheeled into a room quickly.

Carrie tried to call out to Matt, but a nurse calmly told her, "He'll be able to come in as soon as we find out what's going on."

Working swiftly, the medical staff had Carrie settled into bed and started running tests on her. She knew her baby was in trouble and she was scared. She couldn't lose this baby.

When she thought her nerves would get the better of her, a doctor came in and sat down to talk to her. He explained the results of the tests.

". . . severe preeclampsia. We are going to have to deliver this baby now. If not, you could go into convulsions, a coma—you could die, Carrie."

She was afraid for her baby's life. "But I still have ten weeks to go."

"There's a chance the baby will live. We have no time to lose. We have to deliver this baby in a matter of hours. Your blood pressure is still up."

Carrie nodded. "I need to see Matt. Please. He's the man that brought me here."

"We'll send him in." The doctor was gone.

Matt knocked softly before entering the room. "The nurse said they were taking you down to do a C-section."

"I have preeclampsia. They have to take the baby." Carrie adjusted her bed covers nervously. "Matt, Ray is somewhere in this hospital. He was shot earlier. I need you to find him—see if he's . . . still alive. I . . ." Carrie couldn't continue.

"I'm sure Ray is fine," Matt assured her. "He's too stubborn to die. I'll go see what I can find out and then I'll be back."

"No, I want you to stay with him. Don't leave him until he's out of danger. Ray can't be alone."

"I'm sure all of his family's gathered here—"

Carrie shrugged. "I don't care. Stay with him. I can't be there so I want you there in my place."

"I won't leave his side then. I give you my word."

"We have to get her down to delivery," a nurse stated as she eased into the room.

Matt clasped her hand, holding it lightly. "You're going to be fine, Carrie. Everything will be fine."

She clung to his hand a minute before finally letting go. "Go to Ray. Tell him that I love him."

Matt nodded and was gone.

CHAPTER 18

Ray grimaced in pain as he surfaced from the throes of the anesthetic. He opened his eyes and found himself surrounded by Kaitlin, his mother, Garrick, and Jillian.

"What . . ."

"Welcome back, Son. I'm so glad to see those beautiful brown eyes of yours," his mother murmured tearfully. "Oh, thank God. The doctor says you're going to be fine."

Ray's eyes moved around the room. "Carrie. Where's Carrie?"

The room grew silent and everyone glanced at each other. Kaitlin was about to speak up when they heard a sound at the door. She glanced over her shoulder. "What are you doing here?" Kaitlin snapped. "Are you stalking me, now?"

Garrick made a move toward him.

"I'm not here for you, Kaitlin. Carrie sent me."

"WHAT?" they all chorused.

Matt walked up to the bed and stared at Ray. "She wanted me to tell you that she loves you."

"Where is she?" Ray asked angrily. "Why isn't she here

herself?'' He tried to rise but couldn't—the pain was too great. "If you've done anything—"

"I wouldn't do anything to hurt Carrie. Man, you've just had surgery and I'm not here to upset you," he gestured to the rest of the Ransom family in the room, "or anyone else."

"Then why are you here?" Jillian asked coldly. "And where is Carrie?"

"I called her earlier—hours ago—and she was on her way." Kaitlin's tone was accusing. "She would've been here by now unless something happened to her."

Ray's mother held up her hand. "All of you, leave this man alone. Something happened. Matt, that is your name, correct?"

He nodded. "Carrie's here. In the hospital."

"Then why isn't she here with my brother?" Jillian demanded.

"She can't be," he stated. "That's why she sent me. I brought her to the hospital. Carrie is in surgery—"

"Dear God," Garrick muttered. "What happened?"

"Matt, what happened to Carrie?" Ray tried once more to get up.

"I went by your place earlier and I found her collapsed on the floor. It looked like she was trying to get help but couldn't reach the phone. I drove her here—she has preeclampsia. They are delivering the baby by C-section as we speak."

Kaitlin and Jillian gasped loudly.

Ray closed his eyes to the pain. "It's too early . . . I've got to be there—"

"That's why she sent me here. She knew you would risk your life for her and she didn't want that. I'm to stay with you until she can be here herself."

"The baby. It's much too early for the baby, isn't it?" Garrick asked his mother.

Amanda shook her head. "I'm not worried. That baby is a Ransom. It's a fighter."

Ray agreed with his mother. "It's also part McNichols and Carrie's certainly no wimp." He looked up into Matt's eyes. "You don't have to babysit me. You can go."

"I made a promise to Carrie, so you're stuck with me, because I'm not leaving. If you don't want me in your room, that's fine. I'll simply stand outside your door."

A minute grade of respect for Matt showed in Ray's eyes but he said nothing.

"I'll leave you to visit with your family." Matt turned to leave.

Kaitlin walked behind him. "Matt."

He turned. "Yes?"

"Thank you for being there for Carrie. I don't know what would've happened if you hadn't shown up."

"I pray that everything turns out well for them."

Kaitlin nodded. "I do, too. Thanks again."

Matt nodded. "Since you all are here, I'm going back to check on Carrie."

"Do you mind if I come along?" she asked softly.

Matt smiled and her heart skipped a beat. "Actually, I'd like that a lot." Together, they walked toward the elevator.

Ray fought the drowsiness brought on by the pain medication. He was worried about Carrie and their child. He silently prayed that they both would survive.

She sent Matt. Why in the hell would she do that? he wondered. Carrie knew how much he disliked Matt. Just before the effects of the medicine overtook him, Ray let out a laugh laced with pain.

Carrie had sent Matt because she wanted them to get to know one another. And because of their fierce loyalty to her, they would do as she intended. She was determined to have her way in this situation.

* * *

"There she is," Kaitlin exclaimed. "Oh, she's so tiny, Matt." She stood beside him in front of the nursery.

His ice-green eyes rounded in amazement. "She can fit in the palm of my hand."

Tears slipped down Kaitlin's face. "Look at all those tubes sticking everywhere. That poor little baby."

Matt drew her into his arms. "Like your mother said, she's a Ransom—she's going to make it, Kaitlin. I have a strong suspicion, this little girl is going to be a handful. No pun intended."

She laughed. "You're probably right." She brushed away her tears. "You know, this has been one hell of a day. I'm supposed to be on a plane in a few hours, but I don't think I'll be able to sleep at all tonight."

"Please don't go, Kaitlin. I'm so sorry about the way I handled things—"

She shook her head. "Not now, Matt. I can't deal with any more emotions right now. My brother was shot and my niece born ten weeks early on the same day. We don't know if Carrie's out of danger—I can't take anymore. Oh God. Where's Mikey?"

"Brandeis has him. He's staying at the hotel with her tonight. Come to think of it, someone should give her a call."

"I'll do it." She pulled out her cellular phone. "Do you know which hotel?"

Matt told her. He watched her stroll briskly down the hall in search of privacy. Turning back to the window, he prayed for the life of Carrie's newborn daughter.

Ray woke up slowly. He surveyed the room and found Matt sitting up in a corner asleep. He wasn't surprised to find him sitting there. "Matt," he called softly.

Matt's eyes opened and he was instantly on his feet. "Do you need something?"

Ray was touched by Matt's obvious display of concern. "Where's my family?"

"Kaitlin's with Carrie. By the way, you're the proud father of a baby girl."

"A girl. I have a daughter?"

Matt smiled and nodded. "She's beautiful."

Tears glittered in Ray's eyes. "She's okay? She's alive?"

"Yes. She's quite a fighter. Jillian took your mother to see her and then they were going to head home. Your brother went to check on Carrie. Garrick promised to return as soon as possible. I think he meant it as a threat. Your brother, Laine, arrived about twenty minutes ago."

"Laine's here?"

Matt nodded. "He went to grab a bite to eat."

"The food on the plane was terrible and I was starving," a deep voice boomed from behind Matt. "I'm glad to see you're awake. You had Mama and all of us scared to death."

"You flew here from D.C.?"

"I booked the next flight out when Mama called me."

Ray gestured to Matt. "I guess you two met already."

Laine nodded. "I'd already heard a lot about him. Kaitlin had a lot to say about you."

"I love Kaitlin and I intend to make her my wife. I never meant to hurt anyone."

"What does Kaitlin have to say about this?" Laine asked.

"She still feels betrayed, but I'm not going to give up on her. I know she loves me, too."

"Matt, if she doesn't want to be bothered—" Ray began.

"Then I'll stay away. For as long as she wants me to. But it doesn't change anything. I'm sure the two of you want to catch up. I'll leave you to your privacy."

When Matt was gone, Laine turned to Ray. "You know, he's either a big liar or one of the few honest men left in this world."

Ray had to agree.

Matt returned a little while later.

"I went to check on Carrie but she was sleeping."

"I need to see her for myself. Where's Mikey?"

"Mikey's with Brandeis."

"Is that her friend from Virginia? The lawyer?"

Matt nodded.

"I didn't know she was in town," Ray commented.

"She arrived today," Matt offered. "Carrie and the baby will be fine, Ray. Right now you need to concentrate on getting well."

"What I need is to see my daughter and Carrie."

Matt gazed down at him. "Then you'd better calm down and rest. The sooner you get better, the sooner you'll see your family."

Ray glanced at his brother, who shrugged and nodded in agreement.

Matt found Kaitlin just as she was about to leave Carrie's room.

"I was just about to head to Ray's room. I wanted to say goodbye. I'm going home. I still have some packing left to do."

"Why won't you tell me where you're going?"

"Because I don't want you to know. I don't need you showing up trying to persuade me to take you back. It's not going to happen."

"And so you think running away is the answer?" Matt asked. "I know you still love me; I can see it in your eyes."

Kaitlin looked away. "I don't know what you're talking about."

"Please look at me. Tell me that you don't love me and that you want me out of your life. If you can do that, I'll never bother you again."

It was clear to him that she couldn't bring herself to say those words. He was encouraged. "You still love me."

"I'll get over it, Matt." Kaitlin started to walk away.

Matt pulled Kaitlin into his arms, holding her close to him. "I won't say goodbye, Sweetheart. This is not the end of us. I'll find you, no matter where you are. I'll find you and make you mine. That much I promise you."

She glanced around the hallway. "Matt, don't . . ."

He placed a gentle finger on her face as he wiped a lone tear. "I'm going to find you."

"Matt . . ." She started to sob harder.

"Shhh, Sweetheart. I know I hurt you but it was not my intent."

"It doesn't matter anymore. I'm leaving and I don't want to be found. I don't like being used, Matt. And that's exactly what you did. You used me." Kaitlin pushed his hands away. "Please leave me alone. It's over between us."

"I'll let you go for now but I will see you again."

"Don't hold your breath, Matt." Kaitlin turned and fled.

Matt stood staring after her. She was gone, but he wasn't sad. He knew he would see her again. His future was with Kaitlin; he just had to make her see it too.

When he knocked on Carrie's door, she called for him to enter. "How are you feeling?"

She grimaced. "In a lot of pain, but I guess that's to be expected. How's Ray?" Matt could see the worry etched on her face.

"He's fine. Just keeps trying to get up and come see you."

"Kaitlin said the bullet just missed his heart. He wasn't wearing a bulletproof vest. Thank God he's all right."

Wanting to take her mind off Ray's condition, he said, "I saw your beautiful daughter."

"The doctors aren't saying much."

Matt eased down into one of the visitor's chairs. "Carrie, have faith. The little lady I saw in that incubator is the spitting image of her mother. She's a survivor—just like you. She'll make it."

"Matt, thank you so much. For everything. I've put you in such an awkward position—"

He shook his head. "Actually, that's why I came by here tonight. I've caused problems for you and Ray. I don't want to do that. You and Ray are meant for each other. He's a good father to Mikey and now the two of you have a daughter. I'm going to stay out of your lives."

Carrie could see a faint glimmer of sadness in his eyes. "Matt, no. We've got to find a way to work all of this out."

"It's okay. Maybe once you and Ray are married and Kaitlin and I work things out, then I can spend time with Mikey."

"Family means a lot to you, doesn't it?"

"Yes, it does. So much so, that I don't want to break up yours. I'll stay with Ray until you can be there. After that, I'm gone."

"I'm so sorry, Matt."

"I'm not worried, Carrie. Things have a way of working themselves out."

"You've just had major surgery," Matt argued. "Carrie will have me killed if I let something happen to you."

"I need to go to her. She needs me," Ray pleaded. "I want to see for myself that she's all right."

"Are you giving Matt a hard time?" Carrie asked. Allura wheeled her into his room.

Ivy laughed. "You're as bad as Ray. She wouldn't eat until we promised to bring her down here."

"You two are the most sickening people in the world. You act like you can't stand being apart from each other."

With her hands on her hips, Ivy said, "I know you're not talking. You didn't want to leave Trevor and the baby."

Laughing, Ray looked around the room for Matt, but he had disappeared.

Carrie followed his eyes. "Where's Matt?"

"I guess he wanted to give us some privacy. Take a hint, ladies. I want to be alone with my future wife."

"Humph. I could have stayed home with my honey," Allura sniffed.

"See, what did I tell you. All of you are sickening . . ." Ivy complained.

"You're just mad because you and Tony act like you've been married for fifty years."

Carrie laughed as the two argued all the way out of the room. "They are something else."

Ray reached for her hand. "I was worried about you. I wanted to be there—"

"Honey, I know. I wanted to be here for you. I was on my way before things went crazy. Thank God Matt came back when he did."

He gazed into her hazel eyes. "Have you seen our daughter?"

She smiled and nodded. "She's beautiful, Ray. And so tiny. She's not out of danger, but it looks good. I can't wait for you to see her."

"What are we going to call her? We never discussed names."

Carrie closed her eyes and thought for a minute. When she opened them, she said, "I have one. How about Bridget? It means strong."

"I like it."

"And Renee for her middle name. Bridget Renee Ransom." She smiled. "I like the sound of it."

Ray sighed. "I wish I could get out of this damn bed. I want to see my daughter."

Carrie brushed a finger across his cheek. "You have the rest of your life with our daughter. Right now you have to concentrate on getting well."

"I . . . I'm sorry, Carrie, about the way I've been acting. I felt threatened. I fell in love with Mikey from the moment I saw him. When he asked me to be his father—I believe that's the day I did. I can't really explain it . . ."

She nodded. "I understand. But Ray, you never had anything to worry about. Mikey loves you so much and believe it or not, there's enough room in his heart for you and Matt both. But you no longer have to worry about Matt."

"What do you mean?"

"Matt said he'll stay out of our lives. He doesn't want to be a cause of confusion between us."

Ray was surprised. "He said that?"

"He told me last night. From the looks of things, he's already gone. I don't think he'll be back. It broke his heart to do this, Ray. I could see it in his eyes."

"I'll talk to him, Carrie. He doesn't have to do this. I've had some time to think. He's a good man. I still don't like the way he hurt Kaitlin, but he's still a good man."

Carrie couldn't believe what she was hearing. "Do you really mean it, Honey?"

He laughed and nodded. "You really like him, don't you?"

"I can't explain it, but I do. And it has nothing to do with Martin. Matt is his own person. I like him for the person he is."

"He feels the same way about you. He seems to be fiercely protective of the people he cares about."

"So is someone else I know," she teased. "You were ready to kill the man over Kaitlin."

"I really acted like a loose cannon, huh?"

"It's over and done with. However, there is still one small matter: Our getting married. I think we've waited too long—"

"Excuse me." A short portly man knocked on the open

door. "I'm Pastor Bickham and Matthew St. Charles sent me here. He says you two would like to get married."

Carrie turned back around to face Ray and they both grinned.

"Yes, Pastor. We'd like to do it right now, if you don't mind?" Ray responded.

"Wait for us," Allura called out. "You two can't do this without us." Following her were Ivy, Jillian, and their mother. Laine and Garrick strolled in and closed the door. Just as the minister was about to start, Brandeis knocked and entered.

"I hope I haven't missed anything."

"Where are the kids?" Carrie asked.

"They're with Jackson. He flew in this morning."

As Carrie looked into Ray's eyes, she knew they reflected the happiness in her own. This was not the way she'd ever dreamed of getting married, but it didn't matter. They would be a family.

Carrie—dressed in a gown and sitting in a wheelchair—and Ray—in a hospital gown and bedridden—became man and wife.

CHAPTER 19

"Can you believe it? We're finally going to be able to bring Bridget home," Carrie exclaimed. "It's been a long three months driving back and forth to the hospital."

Ray drew her into his arms, kissing her forehead as they waited for the nurse to bring their daughter. "It's over. Bridget will be home with us."

"When are they gonna bring her?" Mikey asked. "I want to take my baby sister home." He paced back and forth across the floor. "I'm tired of standing out here waiting."

Carrie laughed. "They're just giving her a final check-up, Sweetie."

"I wish they would hurry up," Mikey grumbled.

"It won't be much longer, son." Ray ran a hand over Mikey's close-cropped hair. "Garrick did a good job of cutting your hair."

They heard Bridget screaming at the top of her lungs as the nurse brought her to them. Laughing, Carrie reached for her.

Smiling, the nurse said, "Hospital policy. I have to carry this little bundle of joy to your car."

"Okay." Carrie dropped her arms, disappointed. All she wanted right now was to feel Bridget in her arms. She'd dreamed for weeks of holding her baby and not having to return her to an incubator. Now she was still going to have to wait. Her eyes filled with tears of frustration.

When her teary gaze met Ray's, he smiled and mouthed, "It's almost over, Sweetheart." She nodded and reached for his hand.

When they were settled into the car with Bridget in her car seat, Carrie wiped away tears of joy as she felt her baby grasp her index finger. She sat in the back with Bridget, much to Mikey's delight. Like most kids, he loved riding up front.

She had never been happier in her whole life. She and Ray were married. They had their children. Her life was perfect. Carrie had dreamed of this all of her life. Her marriage to Ray was strong. Bridget was healthy. Mikey was happy—nothing could harm them.

Carrie's thoughts drifted to Matt. She hadn't seen him since that day he left the hospital. When she'd tried to call him, she found that the number had been changed. No amount of pleading could force Bob to give her the new number. She was determined not to give up. Matt was now a part of her life and her family. She would not let him just disappear from her life when he'd already pushed his way into her heart.

Carrie hoped that Kaitlin would come to forgive Matt. She knew that they loved each other and that they belonged together. She silently vowed to help them find their way back to each other.

She made a mental note to call Bob and have him invite Matt to Bridget's christening. Kaitlin would be there. Maybe that would give them a chance to talk. Carrie hoped her plan would work.

Matt had kept his word and stayed away. Bob had not been forthcoming about his whereabouts but Carrie was not about to give up.

Bridget was christened on Sunday, surrounded by Stacy, Bob Steele, the Grays, the entire Ransom family, and half of the McNichols family. Carrie was pleased to see everyone getting along so well.

"Carrie, Bridget's getting so big," Kaitlin observed.

"She seems to get bigger and bigger every day," Carrie agreed. She carried a tray of sandwiches into the kitchen. "Did Ray take you by the house?"

Kaitlin nodded. "Yes, I love it. He told me the price you guys got it for. What a great deal."

Carrie set the tray on the counter and turned to face Kaitlin. "Have you heard from Matt?" Since Kaitlin arrived, she'd seemed somewhat withdrawn and quiet. That was not like her at all.

"No," she answered thickly. "But then, he doesn't know where I am. I never told him where I was moving."

Carrie was thoughtful.

Her suspicious gaze met Carrie's. "Why?"

Leaning against the counter, Carrie said, "Well, I've been trying to contact him, but he's not in the same place. Bob says that right now he's in Europe on an extended vacation. He says he's not sure when Matt plans to return."

Kaitlin was quiet.

"You still love him, don't you?" Carrie asked.

When Kaitlin looked up at her, Carrie saw that her eyes were filled with tears. "I'll always love him, Carrie. I just don't think I'll ever be able to trust him."

"Is what he did so bad, Kaitlin? He wanted to be near the only family he has left in the world. In the process, he met you."

Kaitlin shook her head and shrugged in resignation. "I know he loves me."

"Then why not give him a second chance?"

"Give Bob my number in Phoenix. Tell him to give Matt a message. I intend to make him honor his promise."

"His promise?" Carrie was curious.

"He'll know what I'm talking about." She hugged Carrie. "Thank you."

"What are you two up to?" Allura asked as she peeked into the kitchen.

They pulled apart laughing. "Nothing. We're about to clean up—want to help?" Kaitlin asked.

Allura frowned. "Do I have to?"

Kaitlin nodded. "Yes, you most certainly do. Come on. I want to see if Stacy will let me hold my niece. She's a possessive little Godmother."

They all giggled and made small talk as they scurried around the kitchen. Jillian soon joined them. When two of Carrie's sisters offered their help, she had to turn them down by saying, "We barely have room in here with the four of us. Just sit back and enjoy yourselves."

That evening as they readied for bed, Carrie eased up to Ray and wrapped her arms around him. "Today was perfect, don't you think?"

Ray nodded. "Yes, it was. Your family reminds me so much of mine. I guess that's why everyone hit it off."

"I'm glad. I just wish Matt could've made it. I kept hoping that he'd come."

He pulled away from her. "That reminds me. Bob handed me a package before he left. He said it was from Matt."

Carrie took the gift he held and opened it. "Why, it's beautiful." She held up the sterling silver cup to the light. "It has Bridget's name engraved on it."

Ray took it from her and examined it. Placing it on their dresser, he asked. "Did you talk to Kaitlin about him? She seemed to be in better spirits when she left. Actually, she seemed kind of excited about something.''

She nodded. "She still loves him, Ray. She gave me permission to give her number to Bob. Hopefully, he'll contact Matt tomorrow. I think they're on their way back to each other.''

"Kaitlin's flying out tomorrow. I tried to get her to stay, but she wanted to go back to Phoenix.'' He stared off into space. "I wish she'd stay another day at least.''

Carrie was concerned. "What's wrong, Honey? You seem troubled.''

Ray shrugged. "I don't know. I've got a bad feeling. Like something's about to happen.'' He strolled over to the bed and sat down to remove his shoes and socks.

Carrie eased down next to him. "I think you're just tense because it's been a long day. I'm sure everything's fine. I feel like nothing can possibly touch us.''

"I don't know, Sweetheart. The last time I felt like this, my father died.''

"Then we'll just pray for everyone tonight. We'll pray that everything will be fine. We've survived so much already, I don't believe that tragedy will come knocking on our door. Not now.''

Ray kissed her deeply. "I hope you're right.''

Carrie stood up to remove her robe. She wore a black lace teddy underneath. "I think what you need tonight is some good loving.''

Grinning, Ray nodded his agreement as his eyes raked boldly over her. "I think you're probably right, Sweetheart.'' Standing up, he removed his clothes and followed her to the bed.

Carrie crawled in first and made room for her husband. Ray reached for her, pulling her on top of him. Removing the lacy garment from her voluptuous body, he tossed it on the floor.

She moaned as she positioned herself on top of him.

Waves of esctasy throbbed through her as she rode him. His hands reached up to play with her breasts, causing Carrie to nearly lose control. Her lips quivered in unspoken passion.

The hot tide of desire raged through both of them and their movements became frenzied until finally, Carrie cried out and fell against him. Ray's climax followed.

Later, Carrie lay sleeping in his arms, but Ray could not find sleep. He could not rid himself of the deep sense of foreboding.

The next day, Carrie kissed her sleeping daughter before placing her in her crib. Closing the door slightly, she headed to the kitchen to start packing. They were moving into their brand new house at the end of the week.

An hour later, she had most of the kitchen appliances packed away. She heard Ray and Mikey when they arrived.

"You two need to keep it down. Bridget's asleep," she admonished.

Mikey stood on tiptoe to kiss her. "We're sorry, Mommy. Daddy was telling me a joke and it was real funny."

Carrie smiled and nodded. "I'm sure it was, but remember to keep it down."

Ray greeted his wife with a kiss. "It was my fault."

"Yes, I know. And if Bridget decides to wake up, you're the one who's going to get her settled back down."

The phone rang and Mikey answered it. "It's Granny Ransom." He held the phone out to Ray. "She sounds kind of funny."

Ray reached for the phone. "Mama?"

Carrie watched in fear as he closed his eyes and put his hand to his mouth. After sending Mikey to his room, she was beside him instantly.

"I'm on my way." He hung up the phone. Looking down at his wife, he said, "There was a plane crash. It's all in the news. Kaitlin . . ." He couldn't continue. Tears streamed down his face.

Carrie couldn't control her grief as she clung to her husband. "Dear God, no!" He wept aloud, rocking back and forth. She held on to him until he was quiet.

Easing away from her, Ray stood up and went to the bathroom. When he returned, he seemed composed. "We need to . . . to go to Riverside. M-Mama needs us. We . . ." Ray shook his head. "We have to go to Phoenix. Laine is already on a plane headed there."

"Ray, I'm so sorry." Carrie couldn't believe that Kaitlin was dead. She and Matt . . . "Oh Lord. Matt. We've got to get a message to Matt."

Ray slumped down in a nearby chair and sobbed. Carrie wrapped her arms around him, trying to comfort him. Her tears rolled hotly down her cheeks. "Maybe she's not—" She reached for the remote control and turned on the television.

Reports of the crash were on every channel. Then they heard the news they dreaded. There had been no survivors.

Mikey entered the living room. "What's wrong?"

Carrie looked down at Ray. He motioned for Mikey to join him on the sofa. To Carrie, he said, "Why don't you pack an overnight bag for us and get Bridget ready? I want to talk to Mikey alone."

She nodded and headed down the hall. In her room, she burst into fresh tears when she heard Mikey sobbing. How could this happen? Why did you take Kaitlin from us? She silently railed.

She reached for the phone and quickly called Bob. When he came on the line, she told him about the plane crash.

". . . Bob, Kaitlin was on that plane. You've got to call Matt. He needs to know."

"Oh, dear God. Carrie, Matt is on his way home. He left this morning. He's going to be devastated. Please tell Ray how sorry I am."

"I will. I'll talk to you later. We're on our way to Riverside and then to Phoenix."

"If there's anything I can do, just give me a call."

Carrie hung up wishing there was more she could do to protect her family from all this pain.

CHAPTER 20

Carrie moved aside to let Matt into the house. She could tell that he had been crying. She embraced him tightly.

"I came straight here from the airport. Bob met my plane."

"I'm so sorry, Matt. You two were finally . . ."

He moved away from her. "I don't believe she's dead. If she were, I'd know it here." He pressed his hand to his heart. "She is the other half of me."

Carrie thought him distraught. She knew how much Matt wanted to believe that. Kaitlin's whole family wanted that kind of hope, but Kaitlin was dead. Nobody had survived that crash. "Maybe you'd better come in and get some rest. Everyone is in the den. We're leaving for Phoenix tonight."

"I know. Bob told me. I'm going with you. I know you think I'm in denial, but Carrie, I know Kaitlin is alive. I know it. I've heard reports that there are a few survivors—"

"What? When did you hear that?" Carrie asked. Her heart started to thump faster.

"It was just on the radio. There are some survivors. They are in critical condition, but—"

"They said there were no survivors, Matt. Ray and I heard it for ourselves. Are you sure about what you heard?" Carrie asked gently.

"I'm not crazy. I know damn well what I heard. They are recanting the earlier reports. They found some survivors hidden under debris."

Laine stepped up behind her. "Matt, why don't you come with me? You look exhausted."

"I'm going to Phoenix with you all to find Kaitlin. There were some survivors in that plane crash."

Laine glanced over at Carrie who could only shrug.

To Matt he responded, "But the news—"

"Laine, your sister's not dead," Matt insisted. "Call the airline."

"Jillian's on the phone with someone now." Laine shook his head. "Man, you don't know how much we all want to believe that. Matt, I know how much you loved her, but she's gone."

"No, she's not. I'm not leaving Phoenix until I find her."

Carrie took Matt by the hand and led him to the den. Her mother-in-law motioned for him to sit beside her.

As Matt once again insisted that Kaitlin was still alive, Carrie shook her head in sadness. He was in so much pain. And denial. Feeling a need to get away from the somber atmosphere in the room, she strolled outside and sank down on the porch swing.

Ray soon joined her. "Matt's in a bad way."

"I don't know, Honey. I've been giving it some thought—and what if he's right?"

His expression was unreadable. "What do you mean?"

"I mean what if he's right about Kaitlin having survived?"

"Then it would be a miracle. We've had so many miracles of late. Maybe it's just too much to expect another one."

"Ray, I consider it a miracle each day we wake up. Our love is a miracle, and we've been blessed to find each other again. I don't think we should dismiss what Matt's saying."

He seemed to give this some thought. "I love my sister and in my heart, I can't seem to accept that she's gone. But I'm afraid to hope."

Carrie nodded and pulled him into her arms. "Honey, when you lose hope, you risk the chance of finding whatever it is that you hope for. I was at that point when I moved out here. I almost lost a chance at happiness with you."

Ray stared into her medium brown eyes. "I love you so much, Carrie. I don't know what I'd do without you."

Just then, they heard Jillian scream. Ray and Carrie ran to where the rest of the family was gathered.

"What is it?" Ray demanded. "What happened?"

"There are some survivors! They don't have all of the names. The news reports were wrong. There are some survivors." Jillian sank down to the floor. "Oh, Lord, please let Kaitlin be one of them. Please, dear God, let my sister be one of them."

Carrie wrapped her arms around Ray, holding him tight. "I hope Matt's right," she whispered.

Two weeks after the disappointing trip to Phoenix, Carrie and Ray moved into their new house. She burst into laughter as he carried her over the threshold.

"You didn't have to do that," she said as he placed her down on the floor.

"Yes, I did. You're still a newlywed. I would've carried you after we got married but I couldn't lift anything heavy. Doctor's orders."

Carrie playfuly slapped at his arm. "Oh, you are so funny,

Ray.'' She glanced around the room. "We're finally in our house.''

"A lot's happened,'' Ray said quietly, brushing his finger across his mustache.

Carrie felt like a heel. "I didn't mean it that way. I'm sorry.''

Ray pulled her into his arms. "I know what you meant, Sweetheart. It's okay. I'm still not used to the idea of Kaitlin being gone.''

"I know, Honey. Sometimes, I pick up the phone to call her and then I realize . . . she's not there anymore. I prayed so hard for Matt to be right about her being alive. I wanted that to be true more than anything.'' Carrie's eyes filled with tears. "I miss her so much. I feel like I've known her all of my life.''

"She was smart, beautiful, and honest. She was a lot of fun, too. We used to have some good times together.''

"You two were very close. I know your whole family is very close, but you and Kaitlin—you had a special connection.''

Ray nodded. "Yeah, we did. And you know something? I can understand what Matt means when he says that he doesn't feel it in his heart. I don't either. Even though I know my sister's gone—it doesn't feel like it.''

"A part of you is still hoping Matt will find her, isn't it?'' Carrie asked.

"Yes. With all of my heart.'' Ray navigated over to the huge picture window. "Even though I feel that way, I know that I have to move forward.'' He glanced over his shoulder at her. "Our life together is just beginning.''

Carrie joined him by the window. He pulled her into his arms, holding her tight. "I love you so much, Carrie.''

"I know. And I love you just as much. We'll get through this together and with your family. Then, somehow, we've got to help Matt.''

"I don't know if we'll ever see him again. I think when he finally accepts Kaitlin's death, he'll simply disappear. I think it's going to be a long time before Matt recovers—if he ever does.''

Carrie sighed. "I'm so grateful for the time we have, Ray. My life has been so empty without you.''

"That part of your life is over. I thank God for the second chance with you. This is the way it should have been from the very beginning.'' Ray kissed her passionately.

"Mmmmm, I agree.'' She peered up into his face. "Tell me something. Why did you want to leave the kids with Elle?''

Ray grinned. "Because I wanted to make love to my wife in every room of this house. Except the kids' rooms, of course.''

Carrie pushed away from him. "That's a lot of love making. Are you sure you're up to the challenge?''

When he made a step toward her, Carrie ran up the stairs laughing. Taking off his clothes, he chased behind her.

Later, Carrie slept in Ray's arms. He brushed a curling tendril from her face. She moaned sleepily.

"Wake up, sleepyhead. It's time to get showered and dressed. I'm starving.''

Carrie yawned. "Sure, after you rob me of my strength.''

He laughed. "We had a good time.''

She nodded. It was good seeing him slowly return to his old self. Carrie knew he still mourned his sister, and so did she, but they had to move on with their lives. Kaitlin would've wanted them to do so.

Ray scanned her face. "What are you thinking about so hard, Sweetheart?''

"I was just thinking about Matt. He's still in Phoenix, determined to find Kaitlin. He still believes she's alive.''

Ray nodded. "We couldn't even get him to come to the memorial service.''

"I hope he'll be able to find a sense of peace with her death one day.''

Ray nodded. "I do, too. I never really realized how much he loved Kaitlin until now." Caressing Carrie's face, he added, "I think I would be the same way, if I were in his shoes. I wasn't able to let you go in the ten years I was married to Lynette. I wouldn't be able to just say good bye and go on with my life. There would be no life for me without you."

Carrie smiled and kissed his hand. "I would want you to move on, Ray. We don't know how long we have on this earth, but I will die a peaceful woman knowing that I have been loved by such a wonderful man. And when I'm gone, I need you to live on for our children. I'll be in your heart forever always."

"Let's not waste another moment talking about death. Right now, I have this incredible urge to. . . ." His voice lowered to a lust-filled whisper, sending shivers down Carrie's spine.

"Then, by all means, let's not waste another moment," Carrie stated as she pushed away the bed covers. "Forever always," she murmured, as his body imprisoned hers in a downpour of fiery sensations.

Dear Reader,

I hope you have enjoyed *Forever Always*. Most of you will remember Carrie McNichols from *Hidden Blessings*. Look out for Kaitlin's and Matt's story, in 2000.

I would like to take this moment to thank the many readers who purchase and read my books. Your show of support has been overwhelming and I am forever grateful.

I love hearing from you, so please feel free to write me. My address is P.O. Box 7415, La Verne, CA 91750-7415. I will try to answer each letter that I receive. Or you can contact me via e-mail: *jacquelinthomas@usa.net*.

Visit my home page:
http://www.geocities.com/SoHo/Gallery/6681

Blessings,

Jacquelin Thomas

ABOUT THE AUTHOR

Jacquelin Thomas is the author of *Hidden Blessings*. She lives in Southern California with her family. When not writing, you will find her surfing the Internet. She moderates the Color of Love Chat Forum and Message Board, a forum for Arabesque readers.

ROMANCES THAT SIZZLE
FROM ARABESQUE

AFTER DARK, by Bette Ford   (0-7860-0442-8, $4.99/$6.50)
Taylor Hendricks' brother is the top NBA draft choice. She wants to protect him from the lure of fame and wealth, but meets basketball superstar Donald Williams in an exclusive Detroit restaurant. Donald is determined to prove that she is wrong about him. In this game all is at stake . . . including Taylor's heart.

BEGUILED, by Eboni Snoe   (0-7860-0046-5, $4.99/$6.50)
When Raquel Mason agrees to impersonate a missing heiress for just one night and plans go awry, a daring abduction makes her the captive of seductive Nate Bowman. Together on a journey across exotic Caribbean seas to the perilous wilds of Central America, desire looms in their hearts. But when the masquerade is over, will their love end?

CONSPIRACY, by Margie Walker   (0-7860-0385-5, $4.99/$6.50)
Pauline Sinclair and Marcellus Cavanaugh had the love of a lifetime. Until Pauline had to leave everything behind. Now she's back and their love is as strong as ever. But when the President of Marcellus's company turns up dead and Pauline is the prime suspect, they must risk all to their love.

FIRE AND ICE, by Carla Fredd   (0-7860-0190-9, $4.99/$6.50)
Years of being in the spotlight and a recent scandal regarding her ex-fianceé and a supermodel, the daughter of a Georgia politician, Holly Aimes has turned cold. But when work takes her to the home of late-night talk show host Michael Williams, his relentless determination melts her cool.

HIDDEN AGENDA, by Rochelle Alers   (0-7860-0384-7, $4.99/$6.50)
To regain her son from a vengeful father, Eve Blackwell places her trust in dangerous and irresistible Matt Sterling to rescue her abducted son. He accepts this last job before he turns a new leaf and becomes an honest rancher. As they journey from Virginia to Mexico they must enter a charade of marriage. But temptation is too strong for this to remain a sham.

INTIMATE BETRAYAL, by Donna Hill   (0-7860-0396-0, $4.99/$6.50)
Investigative reporter, Reese Delaware, and millionaire computer wizard, Maxwell Knight are both running from their pasts. When Reese is assigned to profile Maxwell, they enter a steamy love affair. But when Reese begins to piece her memory, she stumbles upon secrets that link her and Maxwell, and threaten to destroy their newfound love.

Available wherever paperbacks are sold, or order direct from the Publisher. Send cover price plus 50¢ per copy for mailing and handling to Kensington Publishing Corp., Consumer Orders, or call (toll free) 888-345-BOOK, to place your order using Mastercard or Visa. Residents of New York and Tennessee must include sales tax. DO NOT SEND CASH.

SPICE UP YOUR LIFE
WITH ARABESQUE ROMANCES

WARMHEARTED AFRICAN-AMERICAN ROMANCES
BY *FRANCIS RAY*

FOREVER YOURS   (0-7860-0483-5, $4.99/$6.50)
Victoria Chandler must find a husband or her grandparents will call in loans
that support her chain of lingerie boutiques. She fixes a mock marriage to
ranch owner Kane Taggert. The marriage will only last one year, and her
business will be secure. The only problem is that Kane has other plans for
Victoria. He'll cast a spell that will make her his forever.

HEART OF THE FALCON   (0-7860-0483-5, $4.99/$6.50)
A passionate night with millionaire Daniel Falcon, leaves Madelyn Taggert
enamored . . . and heartbroken. She never accepted that the long-time family
friend would fulfill her dreams, only to see him walk away without regrets.
After his parent's bitter marriage, the last thing Daniel expected was to be
consumed by the need to have her for a lifetime.

INCOGNITO   (0-7860-0364-2, $4.99/$6.50)
Owner of an advertising firm, Erin Cortland witnessed an awful crime and
lived to tell about it. Frightened, she runs into the arms of Jake Hunter, the
man sent to protect her. He doesn't want the job. He left the police force after
a similar assignment ended in tragedy. But when he learns not only one man
is after her and that he is falling in love, he will risk anything to protect her.

ONLY HERS   (07860-0255-7, $4.99/$6.50)
St. Louis R.N. Shannon Johnson recently inherited a parcel of Texas land.
She sought it as refuge until landowner Matt Taggart challenged her to prove
she's got what it takes to work a sprawling ranch. She, on the other hand,
soon challenges him to dare to love again.

SILKEN BETRAYAL   (0-7860-0426-6, $4.99/$6.50)
The only man executive secretary Lauren Bennett needed was her five-year-old
son Joshua. Her only intent was to keep Joshua away from powerful in-laws.
Then Jordan Hamilton entered her life. He sought her because of a personal
vendetta against her father-in-law. When Jordan develops strong feelings for
Lauren and Joshua, he must choose revenge or love.

UNDENIABLE   (07860-0125-9, $4.99/$6.50)
Wealthy Texas heiress Rachel Malone defied her powerful father and eloped
with Logan Williams. But a trump-up assault charge set the whole town and
Rachel against him and he fled Stanton with a heart full of pain. Eight years
later, he's back and he wants revenge . . . and Rachel.

*Available wherever paperbacks are sold, or order direct from the
Publisher. Send cover price plus 50¢ per copy for mailing and
handling to Kensington Publishing Corp., Consumer Orders,
or call (toll free) 888-345-BOOK, to place your order using
Mastercard or Visa. Residents of New York and Tennessee
must include sales tax. DO NOT SEND CASH.*